LEPUS: THE STORY

The world of Lepus the hare is the world of the hunted, the creature whose only refuge is flight. The Creator gave the hare speed and beauty, but condemned him to be forever pursued, and so Lepus is hunted by a variety of enemies from the day his doe brings him into the world—hounds, hawks, and lurchers—but one hunter in particular, Brennan, is obsessed by the black-spined hare. Just as Lepus becomes a legend among the hunters, so Brennan acquires a legendary lurcher, Czar, with a formidable reputation and it seems as though Brennan will achieve his object and take the hare who has so persistently eluded him.

'It requires a rare gift to write a good piece of fiction about animals, especially one in which humans play a large part . . . Brian Plummer . . . knows a good deal about wild life, falconry and greyhound-owner gypsy types and their ways. He is capable of strong and convincing melodrama, too. Everyone who calls himself a conservationist or an animal-lover should read this intriguing and sensitive tale.'

J. N. P. Watson, Country Life

'A remarkably powerful fictional account of the life of a hare—and of the countryside, the people and the dangers among whom it strives to survive. A book, in this reviewer's opinion, to rank with that other classic of hunted endurance, BB's *Wild Lone, The Story of a Pytchley Fox.*'

Charles Roberts, Eastern Daily Press

...AND YOUR NAME SHALL BE HARE

LEPUS
The Story of a Hare

D. Brian Plummer

THE BOYDELL PRESS

© D. Brian Plummer 1981

First published 1981

First published in BOOKMASTERS 1983
by The Boydell Press
an imprint of Boydell and Brewer Ltd
PO Box 9, Woodbridge, Suffolk, IP12 3DF

ISBN 0 85115 219 8

Photoset by Galleon Photosetting and
printed in Great Britain by
St Edmundsbury Press, Bury St Edmunds, Suffolk

British Library Cataloguing in Publication Data

Plummer, David Brian
Lepus: the story of a hare.
I. Title
823'.914[F]   PR6066.L/

ISBN 0-85115-219-8

Introduction

In the beginning, when there was no earth, no sky and no sea, in the Abyss squeaked the animus of amorphous souls, eager to have shape and size and entity. Then out of the Abyss the souls spoke to God, who is called El Shaddai. And the souls spoke and said, 'Lord of All Creation, give us shape that we might delight your eye and walk upon the land you will create.'

And El Shaddai listened. Then from the pit a soul spoke forth: 'El Shaddai, Master of the Blackness, Lord unto the Abyss. Give me voice that with the coming of the morning I can sing to gladden the heart of my maker, so that all things will say, "Look what a joy El Shaddai has created!"'

And God smiled and said, 'Let your wish be granted and you shall be called Lark, and all creatures will gladden to your sound.'

Then the second soul spoke forth: 'El Shaddai, grant me beauty that all might say, "Look at the wonder El Shaddai has given the world!" and let my beauty reflect the glory of the Lord of All Creation.'

Then El Shaddai spoke and said, 'It is good, your wish too shall be granted, and all will know you as Peacock.'

Thus the third soul spoke, tempted by the Almighty's benevolence to the others: 'Lord, I ask for nothing, for I am the meanest of souls, loathsome in my wretchedness. Let me have form and I will content myself with the leavings of beasts, the most wretched of places to call my home. Only, Lord, let me have shape and form.'

Then El Shaddai took pity on the wretchedness of the soul and said, 'So let this be, your lot shall be humble, and your name Rat, a creature of the twilight, content with the deserts of misery.'

But out of the Abyss a soul spoke more boldly: 'Lord, Master of all Things, Mightiest of the Mighty. Make me a miracle of beauty, a creature of perfection. Make my body a delight to behold, my strength a legend, and my speed such that all shall behold and say, "Lo! Not even El Shaddai might outpace him."'

Then El Shaddai shook his head and became wrathful, 'Oh mighty boaster, as I have granted the wishes of others so shall I grant yours. Small shall you be for thus you will not aspire to be a god rather than a beast. Speed and strength shall be yours, for such you asked, and men will covet your beauty. But heed, oh braggart, soul of the Abyss. Heed this! With these gifts I grant shall come bane.

1

Run you will, from the time of your birth till forever, for all shall pursue you, all shall delight in your flight. No place of refuge shall you have until you yearn again for the sanctuary of the Abyss. No hiding place shall be yours and only flight will be your defence, oh boastful one, and you shall be cursed to race your way for all eternity, and – braggart, boaster of the Abyss – I shall call you Hare.'

The doe bore him near to the spot where the blackthorn bushes had burst into flower – white flowers, oddly incongruous against the blackness of the bark – and his birth had not been easy. His sibling had been born an hour earlier, licked and cleaned, hidden amid a tuft of grass near to the smallholding that had somehow eked out a living selling fruit and eggs, dealing in poor, crow-thin ponies. The doe had cleaned the leveret with the oddly unhurried manner which follows the parturition of all her kind. But a collie, kept in uselessness for the holding held no sheep, had disturbed her, and she had fled, leaving one youngster hidden and the second kicking and struggling within her womb. She had run some little distance when the foetus had struggled its way into the birth canal, forcing her to stop, forcing her to pant, to try to lick her hind quarters to assuage the pain of the forthcoming birth.

The doe crouched between some dried and dead thistles and the blackthorn hedge, and her sides heaved, twisting, contorting, not with the exertion of the chase, but with the spasms caused by the contraction of the womb as the foetus struggled its way into a hostile world. She half sat, watching the slithering, wet thing creep from her body, gazing at it as if in amazement, while the head emerged, still covered with the silvery caul of birth. And then, after one violent contraction, the leveret's body and hind legs left the vulva of the doe.

The leveret lay upon the grass, stained and foetid, covered with the bitter, green foetal fluid, and for a while the doe eyed it curiously as if bewildered by the miracle of birth. It was not a new experience to her, for she had seen five seasons on the Dance Estate, and a dozen Jacks had served her, filling her with their seed – seed that had grown into such creatures as had just left her body. The leveret lay still, with no movement of limb, eye or breath to indicate life. The doe began to lick it frantically, nosing the tiny, dark-furred beast, thrusting her snout under him, almost tossing him in the air. The rib-cage fluttered and a tiny bubble of slaver emerged from his nostrils. Her licking became more frantic now, and soon his breathing increased.

She lay back exhausted, occasionally nosing him, licking the sticky fluid round his muzzle and eating the trappings of birth that had accompanied her offspring into the world. He lay there, eyes bulging, a bewildered creature thrust into a bewildering universe. She moved near him, towering over his tiny shape, and he froze – crouching, scarcely breathing, fearful of the shadow of his dam, instinctively knowing that freezing to immobility could ensure his survival over the next few danger-filled days. She lifted him tenderly and moved him away from his place of kindling, a place that would reek of the smell of birth fluid and blood, a place certain to attract the attentions of those whose ways would not be conducive to his survival. The doe carried him as a cat would carry her kittens, gripping him by the folds of skin that hung loosely from his tiny neck. A fox would pause at the place of his birth that evening, sniffing the pungence and the specks of blood that clung to the blades of spring grass, but finding no virtue in the scent would pass on.

The doe tried two or three places to house her babe, but agitated each time by something intangible, she moved him time and time again until she found a tuft of autumn-dried grass that she nosed over him. She stood watching him awhile, as if to ensure that he would not leave the sanctuary of the form, and then left him, ambling away in an unhurried manner, pausing now and again to lick at the discharge that still oozed from her body. She would continue to discharge this bloody fluid a day or more – a time of danger, for scent lies heavy and strong in blood. The doe stopped at a tuft of long grass, yellow and dried by the winds of winter, and browsed, mingling the unpalatable cellulose with the bitter birth trappings in her stomach. Browsing has a curious effect on her and all her kind: a soothing effect, much as nail biting may soothe the nerves of a human during and after times of stress.

She crouched, cat-napping in the middle of the field, eyelids closed, ears held close to her neck, seemingly asleep but ever aware of danger, and she remained thus as the day aged into evening and evening became night. It was time now for her to be abroad, and the pressure of milk within her teats made her remember the first of her young, spawned near the walls of the smallholding.

She sought out the first babe, allowing it to suckle her while she nosed and licked its belly, causing it to defecate muddy pellets of dung – dung which she ate immediately, for dung is scented and a leveret must remain scentless if it is to survive the first days after its birth. The babe sucked frantically at her while she stood, ears erect, as if expecting danger. The collie barked once or twice, disturbed perhaps by the movement of a rat that had eaten its way into the potato pile near the barn, and the doe prepared herself for flight; but

4

NEW-BORN-the dog had always barked at the sound of rats, as if such a gesture was expected of it, so the leveret continued to suckle.

Now that the suckling had relieved the pressure of the milk, the doe felt more at ease and began to browse on a group of rank weeds that surrounded the walls of the ill-farmed holding, pausing at times as if speculating on the nature of some problem; extracting a pellet from her anus to redigest in order to break down the indigestible cellulose of the herbage. It was a necessary action, despised by the ancients, who, unaware of the needs of the body of the hare, declared her flesh unclean because of her preoccupation with her body wastes, disdaining to eat her meat even in times of famine. Those were perhaps the halcyon days of the hare, the days before men became aware that her flesh was good for eating. She browsed and paused, head to one side, as if almost pensive. Could it be that in the quiet times, though hares know few enough of these, a beast may reflect on its past, and race memories come seeping back into the mind.

Her race had known kinder times, warmer lands, when the ice had seized the land on which she now grazed in its vice-like grip, refusing to yield, refusing to melt in the pale summer sun. Her kind had fed below the reaches of the ice and, as the ice had retreated, they had followed it north again, feeding on the plants, the seeds of which had lain dormant beneath the ice for an aeon of time. For a millennium or so her race had followed the receding ice, moving south when the caprices of the weather made retreat necessary.

For a while her ancestors had mingled with other hares, smaller hares, more used to the rigours the Ice Age imposed. These were hares whose coats had expected the severity of the long Pleistocene winter, changing in colour to blend with the frozen landscape, but the species had not mingled and had fed separately even in times of rut, when a fierce madness would seize the males, driving them to mount even the young of their own sex. Thus her kind arrived in the land on which they now fed, lived and bred, and the melting ice had made an island of the land, preventing the retreat south, so that only the fittest and strongest survived the harsh winters that followed the shrinking of the ice sheet.

Foes they had aplenty: wolves, cats, bears, foxes, fed upon their flesh, winnowing out the weak as a sharp breeze separates wheat from chaff, leaving each new generation stronger, faster, more able to survive than the one before. Those slain were the slow, the slothful, the foolish. Those who survived were the fit and the strong. It was a period of savage testing. The Beatitudes are correct – the meek may inherit the earth, but only if they are fleet and wary; and then, irony of ironies, came man, a creature who would trouble, hurt, assail and pursue the hare's already harassed race.

At first the men who came held her kind in awe, a sort of wonder, perhaps a sense of appreciation for the beauty that the Almighty, aided and abetted by rigorous natural selection, had created. The leverets were kept in wicker cages and fed each day by young girls clad in white linen, maids who spoke in soft tongues as if to pacify the wild, untameable beasts trapped within the cages. The spirit of the goddess Lugunda resided in these hares, they said, in voices soft and melodious, and the goddess must be treated kindly. Soft were the voices of the maids and gentle were the ways of the people, but things were not always so, for when drought caused the barley to wither or a blight passed over the pasture bringing murrain to the tiny cattle, the soft-spoken folk took their captive goddess forms and burned them alive, filling the air with acrid smoke and strangely child-like screams. For perhaps Lugunda sometimes needed to be scolded as well as worshipped.

But the time of the soft-spoken folk was drawing to an end, and men with harsher tongues came to the land. These men knew nothing of Lugunda and her magic, they knew nothing of the sacred nature of the hare, nor did they reject its flesh because of its interest in its body wastes. These were men who slew the wolf, the cat and the fox, to become the arch-predator themselves, chasing and slaying the hares with lean dogs, trapping them in nets, rejoicing in the chase as much as in the capture; and the spirit of Lugunda in her wards became a thing of jest, a thing of shadowy legend. For even as the soft-tongued men were driven from the land, so were their gods driven away to be replaced by harsher gods with harsh names and ways, gods who resided in the forms of wolves and bears, ravens and ravenous beasts – and men no longer held the hare to be sacred. The halcyon days were ended, and the hare became an Ishmael, a creature against whom everyone's hand was turned.

Perhaps these race memories crept into her mind as she nibbled at the tough stems of a sow thistle that had grown rank in spite of the severity of the winter, but the urgency of ridding the body of the milk that swelled in her teats and caused her discomfort drove away such archetypal patterns, and she retraced her steps to where her second born lay hidden in a tuft of grass. He froze as she approached, immobile as a stone. No! More so, for it is a gipsy saying that if one sees a shape that may be a leveret or a stone, watch carefully – if it moves it is a stone. She nuzzled him, licking his belly to stimulate his bowels, while instinctively he sought out her swollen teats to suckle. For ten or twenty minutes he frantically drew the fluid from her body while she half stood, watchful as ever for danger. She cleaned him with her rasp-like tongue, shook her coat to rid it of the dew from the long grass, and ambled off. Lepus resumed his stone-like posture.

Night, the first night of a leveret's life, as primeval as the first night of creation, a time of confusion, of rushing sounds, all bespeaking danger. A rat, driven from its lair by a stoat that had taken up residence in a nearby bank, passed close to him, sniffing the air, standing on its hind legs in a comic-book posture to try to detect the presence of the leveret, then scurrying off to feed on some unpalatable filth it found beneath the hedgerow. An owl fanned the air above him, beating its silent wings, feathers muffling the sounds, head alert to detect any movement in the grass below. The owl was certain that his prey lay just below those razor talons, but that which is alive moves, and there was no movement in the tuft of grass. He swung off into the night towards the hedge where the rat snuffled its way through the pile of filth left by a tinker, sifting for anything edible. Lepus heard its sharp, shrill squeal before moth-like wings bore the owl and his prey skywards again. Around him the saga of life and death was being enacted. Next day a village schoolmistress, prissy and inaccurate concerning the ways of the wild, would tell her class of boggle-eyed infants about how kind Mother Nature protected her babes. Fool she would be, for in the field about Lepus the drama of prey and predator was going forward upon the stage of life – a remorseless, pitiless search for an energy source, a soulless, merciless cycle of life and death. 'God sees every little sparrow fall,' the schoolmistress would tell her babes. Then truly tonight the Almighty would witness a saga, a pageant He had witnessed since the beginning of creation: the first night on earth – a time of terror. Then dawn, and the cessation of the predatory chess game where each piece hazards life and death, a time when victor and would-be victim slink away to sleep out the day, ready to resume the drama as soon as darkness falls. It is a night of dangers, thwart with peril, but each and every night will bring such perils throughout the hare's brief and hectic life.

Two nights later, the doe began to visit her second born more frequently. She had returned to feed the first babe, spawned near the smallholding wall, but earlier that evening a rat, heavy with young, desiring proteinous food to nourish her embryos, had come upon the leveret and had begun to eat it, driven to greater fervour by the screams and futile kicks of the babe. The rat had gnawed into the still-living head, eating the kicking, screaming leveret alive, burrowing into its feebly struggling body, delving down into the cooling viscera, skinning the beast and leaving the skin turned inside out like the workmanship of some prankster with a hideous sense of the macabre. The doe had returned that night, sniffed the grass, noting the scent of fear and body fluid, sniffed the skinned carcass awhile, nosing it as if expecting the fleshless skin to suckle her, and then had gone on her way. For a week she would visit the form, expecting to find the leveret each time and baffled by its absence, but after a while she would forget the spot, and when her need to rid herself of milk became imperative she would no longer go to the form near the wall.

Vickery, loosely described by those who farmed the adjacent fields as a farmer, found the leveret's skin the next day.

'Sodding rats!' he murmured, noticing the workmanship of the inside-out pelt, and he kicked the remains against the wall where the ants, warmed by the spring sunshine, would strip it of skin, leaving tufts of dark hair for the wind to disperse around the field. 'Sodding rats!' he reiterated. 'Must poison the buggers' – but he never would. Vickery's life was full of unfulfilled promises, full of *mañana* excuses – a tattered, ill-repaired life, ramshackle as the holding and house he was letting fall into disrepair.

Lepus was three weeks old when the doe visited him but refused his frantic suckling action and plaintive murmurs. She cleaned him, but no longer ate the faecal pellets that contained traces of plant remains now Lepus had begun to eat. She shook him off and denied his need or right to suckle. A week or so before, a young jack, driven into Cotters End by the last hunt of the local beagles, had found her, mounting her many times, filling her womb with his seed, so she no longer felt the pressure of the milk within her teats. She nosed Lepus' anus a few times, licked his ears almost half-heartedly, and left him. He tried to follow her for a few paces, but she was no longer interested in him. A few weeks later she would attack him viciously when he strayed too near the youngster she had just spawned.

Brennan awoke before the birds and rose, cursing quietly to himself. It was his way, and perhaps it always would be. He dressed hurriedly, carelessly, in the manner that would become his hallmark in the nearby village. Brennan – the epitome of the unsuccessful, scruffy school-teacher. He doused his face in the icy water of the cold tap, spat, and cursed again, carefully trying to avoid the mirror.

'God, you're forty and look fifty. Tidy yourself up, you old sod. Take yourself some sane and sensible woman.'

It was a ritual performed as regularly and repeatedly as morning mass, but he would never change. He shaved in the semi-darkness of his tiny kitchen, removing the bristles by touch and intuition rather than by vision, and mused on his life. 'Christ, what a mess!' he muttered. 'What a bloody mess!'

Yesterday he had explained the word anachronism to an un-attentive 4a – 'anachronism', a thing out of alignment with time.

'How about a social anachronism, Brennan, you old bastard?' he said to himself. 'A thing out of place in the profession in which you misappropriate public funds by accepting a salary for the job you are supposed to do. You, who are unable to make a really lasting relation-ship with the countrymen around you in the phoney rural world you have sought to create. You're a phoney, Brennan, a bloody phoney, neither mickling nor muckling, neither horse nor mule.'

Harvey, his settled gypsy neighbour, who visited him each morning, said that in a field where donkeys and horses fed, both kept to their separate pastures and neither allowed a mule among their kind.

'You're a mule, Brennan, fitted neither to a rustic life nor a professional one – a bloody anachronism – a social mule, public-school educated, trained to appreciate Chartreuse in a world where you cannot afford beer, taught to use a rapier in a world where other bastards use guns.'

He shook his head and doused his face again. 'God, what a mess!' he muttered. It was said that a drowning man sees his life flash before him, and every day to Brennan was an act of total submersion in a world he hated. 'What a bloody mess!' he repeated.

His early days had been promising, and his college results had been good, but college days were meant to be an extension of youth, a chance for a man to cling on to a few extra years of Peter Pan existence, and the cold wind of reality had hit him hard. He had character, charisma of a sort, but was disorderly in dress, manner and attitude.

'Hell, I was great at interviews,' he uttered. 'Trouble was, I couldn't do the bloody job when I got it.'

He had drifted from school to school, accepting menial appointments, watching youngsters overtake him in the promotion stakes, allowing his ill-kempt clothes and scruffy ways to make him a figure of fun, no longer seeking to hide his eccentricities and accepting the ridicule, the non-acceptance, the half-hearted persecution of some of his colleagues. He consoled himself with epigrams, not-so-pithy aphorisms to make excuses as to why he just 'hadn't made it' – spiteful aphorisms, vitriolic humour that served to widen the social gap between himself and the rest of the staff.

Women interested him in a way – a brief love affair, and then the disinterest that followed each and every ephemeral relationship nauseated him. Liz had stayed with him for two years, tolerating his odd ways, his dogs, his ferrets and the other accoutrements of his phoney rustic life, but two years was enough to sicken anyone even with the patience of Liz, and after Brennan had flaunted his relationship with a local tart, she had left. 'Christ, I miss you, Lizzie,' he would murmur each day like a priest of Ra uttering a ritual to summon up the spirit of the sun, but it was a fruitless ritual. There would be other women, a host of them, all drawn by his strange rusticism, his odd mixture of classical parlance and earthy way of life; all attracted by it, and finally repelled by it. Living by himself was easier, less complicated, for he was selfish, totally and utterly selfish, and, what was worse, he knew it.

Tea now, copious amounts, libations to the sun just about to rise. "So much tea will damage your liver," one of his temporary lady 'lodgers' had repeated ad nauseam. "Hell, what was her name?" he muttered, he'd thought so little of her. He could remember his 'not-so-funny' epigram about his bequeathing his liver to her to make a pair of shoes.

'Cottage is a mess,' he said to himself. 'Have to get myself another temporary to clean up this sty – looks like a setting for a Ken Russell film on the Black Death.'

He opened the back door and Merab, his lurcher, strolled in, wagging her tail in the oddly unenthusiastic manner which all sight hounds display even when they are ecstatic. Merab – he liked biblical names, a touch of class to the inverted snobbery of owning a poaching dog – a dog that typified a rustic disreputable. Merab, daughter of Lot, though from her biblical goings-on she had little enough class to

11

boast about. 'Probably the original looked and acted like my barmaid woman,' Brennan had thought when he had named the bitch, but Merab had stuck. He poured the remains of his cooling tea into his saucer and the bitch drank.

'You know,' he said, half to himself and half to the drinking dog, 'you're the only female that lasted more than two years with me, and I've no doubt you'd get the hell out of here if you had a better offer.' But he knew his statement was not true. He'd bought her, so to speak, from Harvey, his neighbour, who lived in a cottage as ramshackle and messy as Brennan's became as soon as Lizzie left. Brennan had listened patiently to the lies Harvey told him about how this strain of lurcher had run with his tribe for years before he became a settled man, forgetting that one night, when Brennan had plied him with drink, he'd admitted to stealing the bitch from a council-house tenant just south of Bromsgrove. 'Still, sod pedigree and gipsy lies,' thought Brennan. The bitch had kept Harvey in game for four years or more, and her original owner for a deal longer no doubt, and Harvey valued her enough to beg Brennan to take him by car to a fellow in Norfolk to get the bitch mated. There was a marsh dog, as much collie as greyhound, that was a legend in the district and Harvey intended it to mate his bitch. Merab was the price of the petrol, for Harvey never paid for anything. Everything was either bartered or swopped.

'Make you forget the bloody woman, Brennan,' he'd said carefully, trying not to look Brennan in the face as he'd said it, for the 'bloody woman' had scarred Brennan's soul a mite. 'If I'd my way I'd have no truck with women, Brennan.'

'Then have it,' Brennan had silenced him. 'You're like Cassandra, Harvey, always telling the truth yet never being believed.'

Harvey shrugged, Brennan's classical references always puzzled him and he'd often considered the teacher more than a little mad at times.

Harvey's gift had proved her worth though, and Brennan had had meat in plenty with her and entertainment in excess of the game she caught. She struck down her first rabbit when she was a babe of eight months and caught a hare before she was twelve months old. Though she'd not have been classed as the best in the land, she'd given Brennan rich sport during the dawn hunts that preceded the start of each dreary, pointless, scholastic day. He ran his hands down her flanks, noticing the bulging muscle, feeling the same pride in touching her as Michelangelo may have felt caressing the muscles of his David statue. He cupped his hands under her loins, lifting her hind legs slightly, dropping them again, feeling the muscles of the

12

groin tighten as he lifted her. Brennan, for all his show of culture, which he used against his fellow teachers as a porcupine uses its quills, was a man of simple pleasures, and feeling the muscles of his dog was one of them. 'Keeps lurchers and ferrets,' two of the elderly school governors had sniffed, having made the mistake of appointing him because of his ability to use apt quotes from Browning more than for his appearance or qualifications. But maybe Browning's Andrea del Sarto had felt the same way about the beauty of his 'Madonna of the Harpies' as Brennan felt about Merab. Once he might have tried to explain his odd, oblique sense of aesthetics, his curious pantheism, to people like these two philistines, but now he no longer bothered. He accepted the label 'eccentric', varied a bit by 'lunatic' from time to time, resented it a little, but had learned to live with it.

There was an odd beauty about the dog. She was heavier than a greyhound, black and rough-coated, her back roached slightly, so indicating her power and agility. Her origin was doubtful. Maybe deerhound blood contributed to some of the elegance, perhaps Bedlington terrier blood gave her some of her guts. Indifferent greyhounds had given her speed, and from her collie-blooded sire came a sagacity only found in marsh-bred herding dogs, dogs who could herd, forage and hunt. She would have been quite a hunter if Brennan had had the skill or time to train her, but he had neither, and she was turned loose at day 'to teach herself', as Harvey put it. Twice tinkers had caught her and taken her to a camp ten or so miles away, but she had bitten through the ropes that tied her and returned to Brennan's house next morning. After a while the collie blood in her had made her suspicious of strangers and she gave most men a wide berth. Brennan had lied about her lack of loyalty. Parkes, the farmer from Leeside, had warned Brennan about her wanderings. 'Have to keep her up, Mr Brennan' – teachers, even the scruffiest, were called 'Mister' in Leeside – 'She'll be into the game, and like as not after the spring lambs.'

So Brennan had kept her up, exercising her before the sun had dried the dew off the grass. He stroked her. 'Lo, she is black though comely,' he murmured, repeating the Talmudic quote about the Queen of Sheba, though not remembering where he had heard it. 'Up now, bitch, and away, and sundry mischief to perform. Christ, Brennan,' he chuckled, 'you should have trod the boards, you'd have made a Shakespearian actor – there's a clown or misplaced fool in most of his bloody plays.'

Light was just peeping, pink and ominous. 'Red sky at dawning, shepherd's warning,' flashed into Brennan's quote-filled mind. 'You there, Harvey?' he half-shouted, but there was no need to query it. Harvey would always be there for the dawn run even in summer when the cover made the taking of rabbits a near impossibility. It was Harvey's way to be abroad at dawn. 'Vardo born, vardo bred,' he had said to Brennan, as if he explained a multitude of Romany eccentricities by those words.

The village at large regarded the relationship between these two as incongruous: the almost cultured Brennan and the scarcely literate Harvey. Yet the bond between them was strong. Both were sickened by the social rat-race, worried about the encroachment of the city upon their domains, and both in their own ways were social pariahs. Harvey belonged to the Romany ways of Borrow rather than the life he had known, while Brennan – Brennan was out of place in time and would have been a misfit in any historical era. Still, there was a bond between them and a relationship few, if any, could understand. Certainly Harvey and Brennan could not explain the reason for their attraction to each other.

In spite of Harvey's incessant talk of the old Romany way of life, he had seen little of it. The golden age of the itinerant families had been coming to an end before his birth, and though Harvey had seen the seasonal hop-picking in Kent, the horse sales at Appleby, the making and the selling of pegs, the duckering or fortune-telling, the days of the horse-drawn caravans and the Romany master craftsmen were virtually over, and after his father had died his family had moved 'indoors', taking up residence in a tied cottage and later being housed in a variety of council houses. Harvey still had Romany skills and was able to work well in metal or wood when he wished, but it was seldom that he wished, for that which has a heritage of wandering finds settled life difficult. Brennan often wondered whether early pastoral man ever forsook his herds to take to hunting again, but he never mentioned the subject to Harvey. 'Daft!' Harvey would have said before changing the subject. So Harvey had drifted from job to job, working with animals when he could, labouring when he wished to, and idling his days most of the time.

His tales of Romany life might have been called lies by those who didn't know him, but Brennan understood. They were tales of the life Harvey would have liked to have seen, boasts of days of former greatness; much as a down and out Irishman will claim descent from kings. 'Aye, when my father died they gave him a real gypsy send-off, none of your Gorgio quick jobs. Burned him in his caravan, smashing all his property, killing his dogs, slaughtering his horses and cremating them with him.'

Brennan would listen, nod and understand. It was a shadowy half-truth, a thing Harvey would have liked to have seen. In truth, Harvey's brother had cut the vardo into four, making the quarters into multi-storey rabbit hutches, for wood was scarce in the early days of the Second World War. Thus Harvey's father had been buried Gorgio style in a cemetery near a council estate, but it was not the way Harvey would have liked it. In the evenings after Liz had left, both Harvey and Brennan would stare into the fire and lament their fates, Brennan his failure in the academic race and Harvey the passing of the Romany golden days.

'Craftsmen we were then,' he would mutter, though he would rarely complete any wood-working job he was given. 'Craftsmen! We came from ancient Egypt – Egypt – Egyptian – Gypsy,' he would reiterate, explaining the etymological root of the word to Brennan.

'Bullshit!' the other would mutter, for sometimes the Romany's family stories wearied him. 'Bullshit – the gyps were a tribe from Northern India or maybe Turkey, Harvey. Although, Harvey, you may be right,' he said spitefully, 'you could be right. There are half-finished bloody pyramids all over Egypt.'

Harvey would snort, 'You're a mad one, Brennan, a mad one.'

'Right again, Harvey, right again,' Brennan would agree, fingering the edge of his whisky glass pensively.

'Drink does you no good,' Harvey would utter like an evangelist reformer. 'I had money once, made good money, and pissed it all against the wall.' And after another swallow, said again, 'Pissed it all against the wall.'

'You've a way with words, Harvey, I'll give you that,' Brennan sneered.

'You're a mad one, a mad one,' was always the reply.

There are doubts whether poets ever see the dawn, and if they do they lie about it, for there never was a dawn chorus of the type loved by layabeds like Keats and Shelley. Crows, rooks and magpies chattered angrily at the two men who had no business intruding into the dawn world that birds rightly call their own. A jay yelled abuse twice, causing Merab's ears to raise slightly, and then the bird blended into the cover, invisible among the russet spring leaves of the sprouting oaks. Chance was that neither man would get a run to catch a rabbit this morning, but it was good to be abroad while the world lay sleeping, and both felt a kind of exhilaration about being the only two men in a temporarily depopulated world.

'And all the world to inherit,' said Brennan, shaking his head.

15

- BRENNAN & HARVEY -

Harvey ignored this remark. He no longer listened to Brennan's 'book talk'.

A sparrow hawk – still hunting perhaps, waiting for birds to rise, still dew damp and easy for the taking – flapped above them, catching Brennan's eye.

'Female,' said Harvey. 'Vickery's little bastard shot the musket a week back.'

There was some odd sympathetic relationship between true predators: perhaps a sort of understanding, a sort of *esprit de corps* that only true hunters will understand. Men who rear pheasants as if they were poultry and who ensure that stoats do not touch their rabbits never learn to feel this symbiotic relationship with the predators that harass their wards. Poachers, gypsies and free-lancers like Brennan, however, looked upon foxes and stoats and their kind as fellow predators, cursing them sometimes, but accepting them as part of the rapidly shrinking countryside. A hundred years from now, Brennan and Harvey will be a forgotten race and old men who tell of them will be treated as liars in the concrete jungles that will come to exist where the fields are now – jungles more savage, ruthless and devoid of the code of pity than have ever existed in the history of the land. It peeved Harvey, who was forever lamenting the old times, forever bleating about the encroachment of houses on his own private, verdant little world.

'They're putting a motorway through here next year,' Brennan would tease, and then watch the gypsy's face for signs of anger and choke back his mirth at the tirade of fury Harvey would utter at man and the local council's stupidity. It would come sooner than Harvey or Brennan expected, though; and both would see it in their lifetime – a sight that, oddly enough, would hurt Brennan far more than it would hurt the gypsy.

At Vickery's gate, Harvey and Brennan stood, dogs leashed, gazing across the blitzed, thistle-filled pasture, the hall-mark of an ill-kept farm.

'Don't know how the hell Vickery can scrape a living off this place,' said Brennan, but Harvey wasn't listening.

'Leveret,' he whispered, and Brennan, following Harvey's glance, saw the upright ears of Lepus, who stood ready to run.

'Dark for a hare,' Brennan uttered.

'All leverets is dark,' said Harvey, pragmatic as ever, and then he whispered, 'Jump your dog. Leveret'll do for ferret food.'

Brennan shook his head. 'Harvey, you caused the extinction of the mammoth and the mastodon, I'm sure.'

17

Yes it was untrue and he knew it. Once Brennan had caught a hundred and four rabbits during a night's lamp-hunting with some disreputables and had returned to Harvey exultant as a child with a new toy. Harvey had shrugged his shoulders as he eyed the heap of furry carcasses in the van. 'Great, now all you have to do is to find a family who can eat a hundred and four rabbits. Will you hunt the same land next week or even next month?'

It had been a lesson in conservation for Brennan, and he became mildly embarrassed every time Harvey mentioned the massive over-kill of which Brennan had once been proud. 'Take him, Brennan, he's about a month old. Yer ferrets have kindled and they'll need meat.'

Brennan ignored him. 'Heck, he's dark, Harvey. Black stripe almost down his spine.'

'Plenty of that kind round Dereham,' put in Harvey. Dereham was a casbah, a Shangri-la, a Garden of Eden, a place of wonder to Harvey. His father had told him of it and he'd talked so much about it he hadn't the nerve to tell Brennan he'd never been there.

'One round here now, Harvey,' Brennan had said. 'Maybe more if we leave him. Anyway, he's too small to take. Leave him until leaf fall and he'll be worth running. Take him then maybe.'

'Saying's easy with hares,' said Harvey, crotchety at Brennan's attitude to the leveret. 'Taking's more difficult.'

'Perhaps you're right, Harvey, perhaps you're right.'

Harvey picked up a pebble and tossed it at the leveret. 'Watch the bugger run. Watch him go!'

The pebble landed near Lepus, startling him, making him spring into a run.

'A month you say, Harvey. He's not over-big. I've seen many bigger.'

'Big-uns are easy for catching. It's the middle sods go on to make legends,' Harvey put in.

Brennan shrugged his shoulders. As usual Harvey would be right. Perhaps it would have been better to have slain the infant hare to gorge Brennan's nest of ferrets. The chance was gone now.

And Lo, Fear Came to the Land and All Knew Its Name

It would be known as the time of the drought for years to come, a time of which old men would speak and young men disbelieve, for the old are ever liars in the eyes of the young. It began in the May when the hawthorn blossom had just left the trees, littering the roads with browning petals. Harvey had stared at the stars one night – clearly visible stars in a cloudless sky.

'Bad moon rising, Brennan. Beasts and moons know such things.'

'Moons, Harve, moons?' Brennan had remarked on the plurality. 'Don't tell me, Harve, you learned that saying when the vardo had quartered in some Martian crater. Moons,' he sneered. But Harvey had been right, a bad moon was rising.

No rain fell in June, and the corn on which Lepus had fed began to produce stunted green florets on stunted yellow stalks. The corn would ripen early, though there would be little or no crop. Lepus nibbled the rapidly drying wheat stalks, aware that its short growth afforded him little protection. But the hay grass that grew in nearby meadows was equally stunted and offered even less provender. He had few enemies now, though foxes troubled him somewhat as they stalked him with cat-like stealth when he lay dozing in the hot evenings of the drought. A dozen or more times he was nearly taken, but always, as the teeth were almost into his hide, managed to galvanize into action with a speed that left the fox bewildered if willing to follow a few yards as though to demonstrate a show of supremacy more than a try at catching a fleeing hare.

His body began to flesh out, growing daily, and soon he was a far cry from the bony leveret that had slipped and slithered from his dam near the sloe hedge. His hind legs became heavily muscled, seemingly out of proportion with his body, and his speed and wind increased daily. His fur began to lighten, but the black mark along his spine still remained – a trade-mark, so to speak, one that made farm workers and hunters alike remark that they had seen the black-striped leveret near such and such a pasture. The days were dry, and it would have been good growing weather, ripening weather, crop-raising weather if only there had been rain; but there was none, and the hay grass began to show pollen long before it should have done.

So the hay grass was cut, and for a while Lepus was baffled by the change of the vegetation through which he had run marked and obvious tracks; but the cutting of the grass and its gathering and baling by noisy machinery and even noisier men was a temporary thing, and soon the fields were stripped of grass and silent again. The grasses and clovers which grow after the cutting of the hay came slowly that year, and were less lush and nourishing than usual, but even such sparse nourishment offered more than the fields around, fields where the land was drying and cracking under the fierce sun of early summer. Hares from around the district would converge on these fields to feed, to play the strange, almost mystical games that hares play, following each other in lines, sitting still and watching each other intently as cats watch rats, and then erupting into wild erratic bounds and sudden spurts of running, stopping suddenly to browse on any plant they considered edible.

Harvey and Brennan had watched them one morning, puzzled at the actions of these beasts who seemed to be acting out a scene from an animal Bedlam.

'You know, Harve, a psychologist called Groos says that all play is productive – preparation for future life, helpful to the perpetuation of the species,' said Brennan, suddenly eloquent in spite of his companion's lack of appreciation. 'But for the life of me I can't see how such games prepare a beast for anything.' He shook his head, baffled.

The ancients had watched such gatherings and attributed all manner of human qualities to the hare. 'Hare dances', they had called these games, and during the time of James I, he who had brought the continental madness to the land, a madness that made a puzzled population see witchcraft and demons in all things natural, it was said that such meetings were covens – gatherings of witches who had taken on the form of beasts to confuse the godly, to dance and frolic at the times when good folk should be industrious. It was a time when men reached back to an older tongue to describe such profane goings-on, and forgotten words like were-hares, from the Old English *were* 'a man', returned to the language, and folk, fevered by religion, forsook common sense and dragged old women, scarcely able to hobble, before judges, accusing those who were crippled and addled of being hares; and – madness of madness – such lunacy was believed. It was said by one clergyman, who found the witch-hunting more distasteful than sorcery itself, that those folk who were said to be hares could not be so for the hare had more sense than the idiots accused of such devilry, and, he whispered, more sense than those who judged such fools guilty of witchcraft.

'Can't see any psychological reason for such games, Harve,' Brennan repeated.

'That lot couldn't understand hares,' Harvey replied, then, as a gentle jibe, put in, 'No Gorgio does.'

Brennan groaned aloud, head in hands, and the startled hares dispersed suddenly.

Lepus alone remained, staring as though mesmerized at the couple in the gateway.

'Your jack again, Brennan,' Harvey whispered. That one would always be Brennan's jack from now on – Brennan's own personal property so far as Harvey was concerned.

'He's small for a spring youngster, Harvey, not much meat on him. Doubt if he'll make seven pounds.'

'Sodding idiot won't the way he's going. Won't get much older. Doesn't seem to fear man or dog,' said Harvey.

They studied the leveret a full minute while he grazed, half watching them, half intent on the fading clover that had revived somewhat with the heavy dew of the morning. The dogs on their slips whined softly, tugging to be released, baffled as to why the men allowed such easy prey to remain uncaught.

'You're right, Harvey, the clown just isn't afraid. Any damned cur will snap him up, and he's a sitting target for anyone with a twelve-bore. He needs to know dogs if he's to get much older.'

Harvey bent slightly and slipped the length of binder twine that held his ancient lurcher, and she leaped the gate, her hind legs barely clicking against the wood of the top rung.

Lepus watched her come a moment or so without moving, and then his in-built sense of survival, his fear of anything moving towards him, suddenly mobilized his limbs to action. His hind legs shot him forward, and in seconds he was running at top speed, leaving the bitch far behind. The lurcher was old now, and had never been an athlete even in her younger days, but she knew hares and their ways well enough to realize that Lepus would turn back to the gap in the hedge through which the other dancers had fled. She ran him diagonally now, no longer trying to outpace him, and panic seized him as he seemed to be drawn inexorably towards the gap, the very gap towards which the dog was heading. Fear doubled his speed, and once the old bitch struck at him, her teeth almost touching him, but he ducked and, through the hedge, raced towards the sanctuary of the corn. Both men laughed – more in relief than for the humour of the situation.

'Christ, thought the old girl had him then. Damn nigh had him over then, Brennan. Still life in the old sod yet. Good in her day, best hare dog for miles.'

Brennan brushed the dew-flecked hair from his eyes. 'And lo, Fear came to the land and all knew its name.'

Harvey looked at him blankly and shrugged his shoulders. 'You're a mad one, Brennan, I've always said it.'

They laughed and walked back along the lane to yet another day – a day when Harvey would half-finish a net or so and Brennan would find himself embroiled in the micro-politics which interwove and cluttered each and every scholastic day.

And so fear came to the land, but fear and Lepus' species had long been acquainted, and the dog was just another foe, another enemy, another beast that was to be avoided if possible, out-paced if it could not be evaded. But fear, real fear, the fear that was to make his bowels empty in terror, his bladder release its contents in panic, was introduced to Lepus later that evening. He had fed little during the day and was returning to a patch of clover that lay on the other side of the lane.

The night was hot and sultry, the kind of night that makes all exertion an extreme effort. The night seemingly had this effect on all who walked abroad at this hour, for a car containing a courting couple came slowly along the lane. The hot and sticky night had made the beau torpid and his lady friend somewhat angry about her lover's lack of enthusiasm for the evening athletics that would precede their brief and frantic courtship and their even more brief and frantic marriage. Lepus appeared in the beam of the car.

'Rabbit. No, a deer,' the girl exclaimed as Lepus stretched his body, extending his back legs to race ahead of the light. 'Knock him over, Jackie! Take him home for Dad.' The car accelerated. 'Look at his long ears, Jackie, it's a hare, innit? Go on, Jackie, hit him! Dad'll eat him. They jug hares to cook them, don't they? Go on, Jackie, knock him over!'

Lepus was running now, his heart pounding, his muscles propelling him forward as never before. Panic, blind unreasoning fear, assailed him and he raced between the walls of darkness in the blinding intensity of the corridor of light.

'Go on, Jackie, 'it 'im. Come on, faster. Come on, you're not trying.'

'Christ, he's doing thirty now!'

The car was nearly over him and panic caused his bowels to evacuate. The front bumper of the car grazed him, bowling him, and he was in darkness again, scuttling between the wheels of the car, racing through a gap in the hedge, any gap, any place to escape the brilliant light and pursuing roaring sound.

'Oh, Jackie, you've missed him! Think you got his back leg

though.'

On the car radio a disc jockey with a pseudo-American accent was dedicating a record – 'And now a record for Marilyn – one of the gentle sex.'

'You've bloody missed him, Jackie. Go back, see if there's blood on the road.'

Lepus lay among the nettles, his breath coming in almost a whistle while he tried to turn his bruised body to lick his torn ear. 'And lo, Fear came to the land and all knew its name,' Brennan had said. So many forms of fear, so many names, and all of them Lepus would come to know.

He lay among the nettles for nearly two days, his body too bruised to move. The effort of cleaning his torn ear was an agony, but hares had always cleaned their ears, hares had always been subjected to agony, and so, with paws and spittle, he cleaned the mangled ear every few minutes of the day and night. A fox passed near him, moving quickly, excited by the scent of blood, but excitement is not always the precursor of success in the pursuit of the hare. Lepus lay still, bruised, damaged, a prey easy for taking, but the vixen was a cub unaware of the ways of hares and passed him by. Later that evening, she would become entangled in a snare, an ill-set snare that would encircle her chest, cutting into the rib-cage as she struggled, screaming and bucking to be free of it. She would be petrified and fearsome when the youth who had set the snare checked it the next afternoon. For a while he would walk round her, watching her insane gyrations as she tried to turn to face him, and then, tiring of his sport, the youth would find a stick and kill her. It would take many blows to do so, and in the awful rictus of death her teeth would become embedded in the branch. 'Cub,' the youth would mutter and kick the carcass into a ditch. 'Skin's worth sod-all.'

A badger would snuffle past him, as blind at night as she would be by day. That evening she was full of bluebell bulbs she had dug from the hard-baked clay at Meachams Bank, a meal she had used as a dessert to the half-rotten rabbit she found near her set. The sow smelled him, but was unsure of exactly where he lay, hidden in the nettle patch, and she had snuffled and grumbled her way back to the set, for dawn was rising and it is a bad thing for a badger to be abroad during hours of sunlight. Three days after the incident with the car, Lepus was able to run again, though he carried a limp for several days. A limp is an ill thing for a hare at the best of times, and this was not the best of times, for four days later the corn was cut, and fear came to the land and all knew its name.

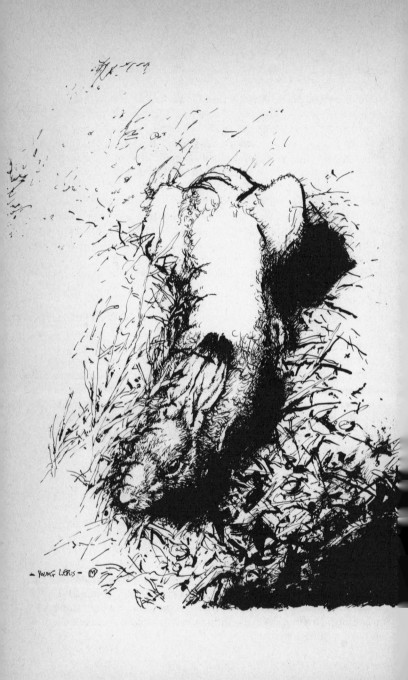

— YOUNG LEPUS —

So the corn was cut and the myriad beasts would awake to their last dawn, for with the cutting of the corn came a ritual, a ritual associated with the harvest, a ritual not designed to assuage the fury of the gods of the granary, but one to satisfy the viciousness of men, for the harvest invited the hunters, enthusiasts eager to blast to death all those who had found shelter among the browning stalks, men eager to slay all those who now crouched trembling in the dew-dampened fields. A mixed collection of folk would come to shoot the fields, now being reaped and raped, harvested by the noisy machinery, men ill-at-ease with country ways, unskilled in bush craft, untutored in the ways of the wild: a mixed bunch gleaned from every walk of life, but having as a common denominator an interest in shooting and a desire to ensure that death would brighten the days of the fast fading summer.

They had shot this farm a dozen or so years now, leaving a swath of destruction each and every season. Three thousand years before, these fields had seen the slaughter of sheep and goats, victims to ensure that the goddess of the corn would smile upon the grain-gathering folk and give them bountiful harvests. Beasts would be slain and their blood would dapple the reaped fields, for gods and men delighted in blood, it was said. With the coming of the white Christ, men forgot their savage ways and no longer slew the best of their herds to please the field goddess, and the earlier deities of the land slumbered and slept. Today, however, would witness a similar blood-letting, a similar offering to a deity, a deity that all those who should have known better would call sport. Today would promise enough slaughter to appease the most bloodthirsty pagan deity, to satisfy a Moloch let alone a Cybele, for today the corn would be cut and the sanctuary that had housed a microcosm would be removed and there would be no place for the wild things it held to hide. It would be a day like any other day, yet unlike any other day the dwellers in the corn would know.

Men stationed themselves around the field along the hedgerows, eagerly awaiting the approach of the harvester, and they crouched among the foliage of the hedge and waited. Brennan, whose summer vacation was drawing to an end, watched and sighed. They were intruders, these town dwellers, men who disturbed his solitude, upset the equilibrium of his lonely life. He watched, shrugged and shook his head.

'And there came strangers to our land and they knew not our ways,' he muttered and turned away.

A dozen years he had witnessed this ritual, a dozen years he would be sickened yet incapable of stopping the seasonal massacre.

'I am a king of a rainy country, rich and impotent, young yet very old,' he murmured each and every harvest time, for Brennan, like Baudelaire, was a paradox – both men rich in poetry and little else. He would go into the village today and remain there, staying until the corn was down and the hunters gone from the countryside, for then tranquillity would return to the land. He felt bitter about the intrusion of these men, bitter that they would hunt his fields, slay his game, litter his lands with cartridge cases and useless cadavers. But then Brennan would always find himself in conflict with his environment, for it was Brennan's way to be so. So Brennan walked to the village each harvest day and stayed there until nightfall. He would waste his day trying to seduce a shop assistant, trying and failing, trying without really wanting to succeed, but today any place was better than his cottage adjacent to the corn fields.

So the juggernaut of the harvest cut the first swath of the corn, showering the grain into the grain trailers and driving the timid dwellers of the corn further into the field. A second swath and the gunmen slipped the safety catches on their weapons. A rabbit ambled slowly out of the corn towards its burrow in the hedgerow across the yard of uncultivated land that separated the corn from the hedge. A short dash, almost a leap, but one he would never complete. An explosion and the cry, 'Yours, Johnson, I think. It's a small bugger. Leave him – not worth taking. For Christ's sake, stay in position, leave him. If you move now you'll miss the fun.'

The rabbit thrashed a while, its hind legs drumming on the dry soil, its eyes blinking wildly. 'For Christ's sake, Johnson, stay in position. Leave the little bugger, it's sure to die. You've gut shot it.'

It thrashed furiously now, reluctant to die, refusing to expire, believing it would find sanctuary in the shade of the hedge; but the hedge was far away now. 'Stay in, Johnson. There'll be more coming now.'

The rabbit stopped thrashing and its eyes became fishy, sightless, lifeless.

Another swath of corn fell before the reaper and the sound of gunfire became spasmodic as various creatures made a mad and fruitless dash for sanctuary. A rat, pregnant as are all doe rats in summer, slithered out and fell before the blast, a blast that lifted it clear of the ground, a blast that tore slivers of flesh and fur from its

26

body, bowling it over, killing it instantly; yet the tail refused to die and twitched a dozen minutes or more.

'Pheasant, Johnson. Sod the season. Hell, he's mine then. Melanistic – Christ, he's a beauty!'

It was untrue. Once he was a beauty, now he lay, plumage speckled with blood and the feathers oddly less iridescent than they had been a few seconds before.

'If you wait for the bloody season you'll get sod-all, Johnson. Wits about you now. Yours I think. Good shot, man.' And a wood pigeon fluttered to the ground, crumpling like a damaged kite, crashing back into the still-standing corn.

Panic had now seized the fox cub that lay in the centre of the field, and he padded his way through the stalks, restless, wide-eyed, dog-like, yet with the ways of a cat.

'Fox or cat, Parsons?'

'Fox, I think, Johnson.'

'He'll be back. He's not going anywhere. There's nowhere to go.'

Johnson laughed at the absurdity of his joke, but it was true. There was no place to go. Once panic had mastered discretion, the cub would dash for cover, but it would be a fruitless dash. They would bone his scrawny cub's tail, keeping the brush as an ornament; one that Parsons would give to the girl who worked in the transport café as a curio – a curio she would throw into the dustbin that evening because it stank.

'Where there's one, there'll be more,' shouted Parsons. He knew. He had murdered on these fields for four years now.

Moorhen now scampered their way out of the corn, running like pregnant washerwomen, and small birds took to the air. Johnson, elated by his first kill, aimed and fired at close range.

'Christ, Parsons, d'you see the way I smashed that black thing? Point-blank bloody range – not much of it left now. Christ, what a shot! What d'you call those little black things?'

It had been called a moorhen once; now it was a shattered, bloody mess, the feathers of which protruded at obscene angles from the mangled carcass. 'Christ, you should have seen that shot, Parsons. Not bad for a beginner, heh?'

'Wits about you, Johnson, you've seen nothing yet.'

A leveret had panicked, terrified by the fury of the harvester, and dashed hither and thither, mindful of the men around the field shutting off its escape. Back and forth it ran, and finally in panic it crouched – crouched as had the terrified members of its tribe since time began – crouched to escape, to be unnoticed, to be overlooked by predators. Harvesters are remorseless hunters, unpitying predators, and the blades tore the crouched beast almost in two – macerating – crushing – splintering the tiny body, drowning its death scream in the furious sound of the mechanism.

'See that, Johnson? Bloody waste that. I hate bloody waste. Pointless killing.' The moorhen was attracting blow flies now. 'Cut the little bugger in two. Rabbit or hare, dunno which.' It would take an expert to know now.

'Crow, Johnson. Shoot the sod! Bloody vermin!' The black shape squawked, fluttered, regained height and was brought down by the second barrel. 'Bloody vermin! they destroy game, you know. When you've shot this land as long as I have you'll hate the black sods. They've no place in our ecology, the murdering bastards.' Oddly, there was no trace of irony in his voice.

The sanctuary was shrinking now, a haven only for the most timid, the most frightened, and still the slaughter continued until the last stalks fell to the reaper's blades. 'Thanks, Mr Harrison,' Parsons had said to the farmer. 'Bostin' day, the bloody barrels are damn nigh red hot.'

'Coming again, Johnson?'

'Try to stop me. Next year, Mr Harrison, next year then,' and the cars roared towards the town again.

That evening Harvey walked the fields, silent as only Romany folk can be. His lurcher bitch nosed out the dead crow from under the stripes of cut corn stalks, retrieving it to Harvey. 'Ferrets'll eat it,' Harvey said, 'as well as this little drummer,' and he pocketed the diminutive rabbit. He eyed the cut fields and the carcasses of the slain. 'Bastards!' he muttered, 'Bloody bastards!'

Near the hedge some wasps, carnivorous as wolves, were stripping meat from a tattered mess of flesh, feather and bone. They buzzed angrily as the lurcher approached, and she heeded their warning, skirting them, leaving them to their grisly feast. The wasps continued to burrow and buzz into the shapeless mess of black feathers and meat. Earlier in the day it had been a moorhen.

Harvey touched the chain and the gate yawned open. He slid into the field almost fluidly, blending with the hedgerows instantly, becoming a part of his surroundings. 'Christ, he's furtive, even when he has permission on the land. A natural skulker,' mused Brennan.

'The silent people,' the Gorgio had called Harvey's band when they first came to these islands, and the gift of becoming unnoticeable was still with Harvey. He moved silently, talked little and quietly, and in spite of his predatory ways he occupied an ecological niche, blending into the countryside, becoming a part of whatever landscape he walked.

'Christ, I've never blended anywhere, never been part of any entity,' thought Brennan despondently. 'When you get to those Pearly Gates you'll just slink in, you old bugger,' he muttered as he eyed his companion.

To every action there is an equal and opposite reaction, Newton had said, and it was this rule which probably accounted for the relationship between the two.

Brennan closed the gate and slipped into the field where the undersown grass had begun to flourish now the corn had been cut, oddly lush, as if unaware that winter had just arrived. The gate creaked slightly and Harvey turned, his expression pained at the unnecessary sound Brennan had created. A blackbird, roused by the sound, screamed alarm to all those foolish enough to be still abroad at this early hour.

'They've been feeding here two weeks or more. An old jack, I think, and two or three does. Seen your black-striped leveret here, too, excepting he ain't a leveret any more. He's a jack now. Small, but still a jack, and able to run as well as most you may be sure.'

Brennan stooped and unslipped his lurcher. She viewed the field, staring hard to detect any movement in the grass. Eventually, she began to cast around, aimlessly at first, unable to find traces of huntable quarry, but finally running a line with that quiet, almost reserved enthusiasm which all sight hounds seem to possess. She began to quest eagerly, certain that runable quarry lay hidden out in the short grass.

'One about, Harvey. I'll put her on the slip and walk up the sods.'

'Care about the slip, make it a short one, Brennan. A long slip will find her buggered and she'll go home with her arse in a sling and nothing to show except a bad blowing. Walk her up slow. Choose your slip carefully. Hares round here are strong this time of year and take some running, though they'll be stronger still next side of Christmas.'

It was at that moment that Brennan glanced up and saw Lepus.

The hare sat quizzically in a patch of dying ragwort, browsing on some dried grass, watching Brennan with the air of casual indifference that is characteristic of his kind. Ears flat to back now, then erect, as if not totally certain whether the approaching figures meant him harm, certain and yet uncertain that no beast could possibly chase and capture him. He browsed nervously, a gesture he would always perform whenever uncertain or upset – it was the way with all his kind.

Brennan watched him for thirty seconds or more, bewildered at the beast's indifference to danger, wondering whether there could be mentally defective hares just as there are mentally defective humans, and then he began to walk almost casually towards the feeding hare, who eyed him, head turned to one side, more like a Walt Disney caricature than a real creature. The distance between the protagonists narrowed. Eighty, seventy yards, and still the hare continued to feed. Brennan sensed a stiffening in the dog, the almost imperceptible tension that somehow ran like an electric current up through the slips, causing Brennan's arm to tingle. Closer now, and Brennan began to stalk the seemingly half-witted beast in an insane parody of stealth.

Insane it was, for Lepus had been aware of him for the last half mile, had listened to his noisy, clumsy footfall for twenty minutes or more. He knew dogs, farm dogs, curs who had chased him. He knew them well enough, knew their measure, their weaknesses, knew them well enough to realize he could outpace them whenever and wherever he wished. He was almost contemptuous of them; that is, if contempt can exist alongside the fear omnipresent in each and every hare. For a while, flight would be unnecessary, and he continued to browse, ever watchful of the approaching dog. Thirty yards now, and Brennan reached down and slipped the dog Merab. It was then that Lepus moved.

He moved, no, he erupted, and instantly Brennan realized why poets had sung the praises of such creatures in tongues spoken at the dawn of time. He moved and exploded into flight, and the dog, startled somewhat by the rapid explosion in the grass, was left far behind. Merab knew hares, however, knew their first sudden flight, knew their speed, their cunning, their sheer audacity that could turn obvious capture into ridiculous, foolish defeat, and in seconds was on the racing, diminutive form. She was heavily built for a lurcher, but such a build is deceptive and hides a power-house of muscle; and she was old to the ways of hares since she had run them, and run them well, for three seasons now. She closed with him again, and struck at him as he weaved left and right to avoid the jaws that reached down to him, dappling his coat with hot, wet slaver. He kinked, throwing his body sideways as only a hare can do, and the bitch careered on, losing ten yards before she turned. Ten yards, a fraction of a second, but respite enough for a hare to ensure that capture was not inevitable. But there was no respite, Merab was on him again, striking at the weaving, bobbing shape that tantalizingly evaded her bites. Brennan watched, mesmerized, as enchanted by the magic of the chase as he had been at the sight of his first course. Merab turned Lepus and he raced back towards the men.

'Christ, look at them, Harvey. It's like aiming at a shadow,' Brennan uttered, and Harvey nodded.

To the casual observer, those not used to the ways of hares, it was a strange contest: a forty-pound dog, a miracle of beauty and grace, against a tiny, seven-pound, hump-backed hare. It was an uneven contest, but Lepus knew his own ground well enough. He knew every tussock of grass, every weakness in the hedge, every vantage point where he could confuse or bring down a dog. This was his chess board, and it was his advantage to move the pieces where and when he wished. He jinked at a hollow, throwing himself beneath the pursuing bitch, causing her almost to topple as she struck at him as he passed between her legs, her clumsiness causing the distance between them to widen. Then she was on him again – relentless as death itself. His bladder and bowels evacuated and the scent of fear and filth intoxicated the bitch, making her efforts fourfold to catch the dancing, weaving creature that somehow evaded her; but, at the very moment when capture seemed certain, he slipped through the pig wire and was away into the ill-kept, thistle-filled fields of the Vickery pasture, towards the meadow edge that housed the tangle of wire and rubbish which had lain there since Vickery's demob in 1945. Lepus headed towards the thicket.

It was more a tangle than a thicket: a mess of wire, more oxide than metal, that had lain there rusting for twenty years or more, and it had been a sanctuary for wild life since Vickery, casual as ever, had tipped the rubbish there, hoping, just hoping, that some tinker or scrap-metal merchant, eager to make a few pounds, would find the muddle of farm implements and wire attractive enough to remove without costing Vickery effort or money. No one had found the rubbish worthwhile, so the heap had become overgrown, tangled with bramble and cleavers, a haven for rats, mice and birds. A fox had lain up there a month ago, panting hard, snarling, fearsome and fearful of the hounds that had run him to the edge of Vickery's plot, hounds that were whipped off there, for Vickery found the gentry and their obvious distaste for his hovel offensive and refused hounds on his land. Rabbits had bred there last season amid the piles of rusting iron struts that had once been one of those pieces of antique farm machinery quaint enough to confuse experts as to its function, but the rats that were part and parcel of Vickery's farm had devoured the young rabbits so often that the does had become agitated and moved elsewhere. It was for this tangle that Lepus was heading.

Merab closed with him once more and struck, and he rolled to avoid the collision, scarcely altering his speed as he regained his feet again.

'Christ, she's got him,' Brennan yelled triumphantly. 'The old sod's got him, Harvey.'

'She ain't,' muttered his associate. 'He bowled, and she's missed the strike as he went over.'

Again she was upon him, aiming blow after blow at him as he neared the thicket. She was frantic now, her waning stamina taxed to the full as she tried desperately to turn him from the tangle. Twice she turned him, and twice he evaded her *coup de grâce*. Suddenly he jinked sidewards and was into the thicket, and the dog, driven on by her own impetus, careered in after him.

Brennan heard the scream from two hundred yards away, and raced to the thicket. Merab stood there panting, blood streaming from a dozen cuts, blood oozing unhurriedly, covering the black fur. She limped badly, winded by the collision, and her breath came as almost a scream.

'Put your thumb on the leg wound or you'll bury the bugger. It's through to the vein here. Forget the other rips. Stop this one bleeding or she'll leak to death.'

'Bad wound in the belly, Harvey. Dogs die easy of belly wounds. You told me they let in the badness.'

'Forget it, Brennan, staunch the leg wound. Under my thumb here.'

Brennan thumbed the vein. 'Christ, a vet will need to be a jig-saw puzzle expert to put this one together. What a mess! What a bloody mess! God, did you see him go, Harvey? Thought she'd got him then – had him once or twice. Hell, what a hare! What an athlete! Did you see him go? Jesus, what a beast! Run him again and get him next time, you'll see.'

'Not with this bitch, Brennan,' Harvey put in almost spitefully. 'Not with this bitch. Her tendons are cut.'

The winter came suddenly, so suddenly that even Harvey, arbiter of the ways of weather, did not foresee its approach. One morning, as he and Brennan returned from a fruitless hunt on which they had taken the ancient and crippled lurcher, Harvey spoke. 'Listen to the mistle thrush, Brennan. He's shouting loud. Calling up a storm. A heller this one will be.'

Normally Brennan would have ridiculed it, as he did all Harvey's superstitions, but the sky was indeed leaden grey and the clouds pregnant with snow.

'Be a heller. Wait and see,' said Harvey. 'Listen to the fields. Apart from the storm cock's warning the fields are silent. Beasts know when bad weather's coming up. Hear the silence, Brennan.'

There was a fluttering as the crippled lurcher chanced on a woodcock that rose reluctantly into the darkening sky.

'Even those'd sooner sit than fly, Brennan. Most times they'd be up and off before a dog winded them. Beasts sit tight to weather a storm rather than fly or run. Best to be in and dry, covered over, than chancing a storm.'

'You're rambling again, Harvey,' said Brennan, irritable as ever about the life that forced him to leave his solitary cottage to teach in the nearby town.

It was noon, however, before the force of the storm hit and the sky began to shower down tiny fragments of half-frozen snow: snow that stuck to the frosty ground, refusing to melt, fine light snow that swirled and drifted, filling crevices, creeping in through the gaps in Brennan's ill-made window frame; snow that littered the wash basin in his stark bathroom-cum-kitchen. Outside, a rat that lived in the tiled roof of his cottage scurried around the house, leaving star-like footprints – footprints that vanished under eddies of drifting whiteness.

In the field nearby, Lepus, crouched in a clump of grass, rump to the wind, ears held tight to his back, was sitting out the storm, his fur set to trap any warmth against leaving his body. He shook his fur from time to time lest the melting snow should wet it, and stared as though dazed at the drifting eddies that danced on the surface of the hardening snow. It was a good thing to sit out a day like this, a good thing not to be abroad at such a time, but that night there was no abatement in the storm and the freezing snow continued to increase in

33

depth. His belly became empty, filled only with the faecal pellets he had reingested – a second chance to glean any value from the coarse cellulose of the dead grass eaten just before the storm struck. It was a time to sit still now, though, a time when it was best to stay quiet and conserve energy rather than waste it foraging abroad for provender. 'The hare limped trembling through the frozen grass,' Keats had said, but tonight it was best not to venture abroad.

A vixen passed him late that night, hunting to fill her empty belly, a belly that had been empty for two days after her paw had been pinched in a gin trap set unwisely by Vickery – a trap set for rats in a place where rats were unlikely to run. The vixen had been drawn to Vickery's stinking midden pile: a pile of filth littered with dead battery hens – ill-husbanded birds who would have lived out their lives in splendid confinement had not Vickery tampered with their diet, mixing his own meal to skimp a penny or two, leaving their food deficient in vitamins so that no eggs came and they found the flesh of their fellow prisoners a suitable source of the vitamins he denied them. Thus they had jostled, pecked and prodded various members of their fellow captives to death, and had continued to peck at the carcasses until only bones and feathers remained – unsuitable food even for a starving hen. Vickery had thrown the bony mess on to the midden pile, lamenting his ill-luck rather than his bad stockmanship, for Vickery attributed all his problems to bad luck.

For a while the rats, Vickery's ever-present guests, had gnawed the flesh that still clung to the bones, inspiring Vickery to one of his rare bursts of energy, and that morning he had set the yard bristling with gin traps brought out of retirement to do illegal battle with vermin. No rats had been taken, but that evening the vixen, moving foot before foot, elegant as a ballerina, cautious as a virgin, had chanced on one, and the teeth of the gin had bitten into her paw. She had snapped at the iron trap biting into her toes, splintering her teeth, tearing her lips and gums, and eventually, in agony, she had bitten into her own flesh, leaving a piece of the severed paw still locked within the teeth of the trap.

'Sodding foxes,' Vickery had said, ghoulishly and gleefully, noting the fragment still caught in the trap. 'Wish it had been a whole fox. A skin's twenty quid these days. Still, I'd have to skin the bugger,' he comforted himself, 'and take it to town to sell. Waste of time, really,' he muttered, scratching at his scabrous midriff.

The vixen's foot had swollen rapidly and the agony had been intense. For a week or so, she would come down to feed on the midden pile, hunger conquering the fear of the traps, and eke out this pitiful food with the rats that were fellow foragers on the heap. A few days later, frost and filth would conspire to turn the wounds gangrenous and she would fever to death in an earth on the railway embankment; her mummified body, minus a foot, becoming a source of amazement to two farm lads out to dig foxes with their terriers early next spring. Now, however, she passed near Lepus and sniffed the air, the snow baffling his body scent. She stood almost on hind legs to detect his presence, and then loped off towards the midden pile and more certain food, urinating at a crouch a yard from where Lepus lay.

Brennan walked home that night, leaving his car in the nearby town.

'God, it's cold, Harvey, bloody cold! Maybe I'm getting old and can't face the weather. Forget tomorrow morning, give it a miss this week.' He gazed through the window at the snow stinging the window panes. 'He's out there, Harvey, weathering out the cold, the little sod. Let's hope no one takes him. He's mine by rights now.' He said it almost bitterly.

'Bad thing for a man to be at war with a beast,' said Harvey. 'Seems a mite ungodly.'

Brennan laughed. 'I'm hardly any bipedal Captain Ahab after a furry Moby Dick, Harvey.'

Harvey shook his head, not understanding nor appreciating Brennan's sudden eloquence.

'With the spring I'll buy another lurcher and get him. God help me if I don't.'

'Who'll sell you the beast good enough to take him? Beasts of that ilk are bred not bought. Even when they're bred they're never sold.'

But Brennan, gazing out into the blackness, was not listening. 'You'll see, Harvey,' he muttered, clutching his cup. 'You'll see.'

Later, on his own, he suddenly felt alarm at his growing frame of mind. 'Snap out of it, Brennan, for Christ's sake,' he told himself. 'You'll finish up like Melville's Ahab, conducting a personal vendetta against a bloody dumb beast that merely tried not to get caught. You've been in the wilds too long. You're getting more like an animal by the day.' He shook himself out of his reverie, determining to join a club, to maybe meet some woman and expand his social life. 'Some sort of a lunatic you're becoming, conducting a blood feud with a beast. Snap out of it. You're supposed to be a cultured man.'

Next year, though, he would seek out a lurcher fit to hunt the hare.

For three days it snowed and the traffic slithered to a halt. Snow choked the roads, making rough places smooth and bushes into white cotton-wool balls. On the third day the snow abated and the frosts came, rendering the snow crust-hard and brittle, sharp and jagged to the beast who broke through the icing-sugar surface. Lepus was weak and chilled as he limped his way in search of food. He paused momentarily to rasp the bark from a hawthorn hedge, gnawing into the bitter woody tissue to assuage the emptiness of his belly. The bark's sharp acidity burned within him, mingling with his stomach juices, filling him but refusing to yield up its goodness. He nibbled at the tips of the long dried grass that stood above the snow line, and belched acidic gases. Overhead hung the dried, shrivelled carcasses of the larder of a shrike, the shy, curious bird who impales its victims on thorns for some future repast, though the meal is often forgotten in the golden worm-filled days of summer. Now the grisly trophies hung, dried and frosted, swaying stiffly in the chill breeze.

High above Lepus a wood pigeon flapped its way, casually, noisily, unhurriedly in search of plant food of any kind. Before the coming of the snow she had been fat and acorn-filled, for there was food in plenty with the land being shot regularly and fewer of her kind to feed on the great crop of acorns that autumn produced, mindful perhaps of the coming rigours of the winter. Three days of fasting soon reduced this fat, and her mutes were green, for the liver was depleting the last of its stores to ensure her survival. She would survive the winter, feeding on sprouts and kale, emerging herring-thin in the spring. She would survive, this most persecuted of birds, shot by all regardless of season, yet still common enough to baffle ecologists as to the reasons why such a bird should not be extinct. She would survive, yet the winter would tax her sorely, and many of her kind would flounder in the snows, too weak to fly, before the winter released its iron grip upon the land.

It might have been the *fimbul* winter, the ice age that will precede the ending of the Viking world, a three-year winter of ceaseless frosts and snow storms. The sun burned pale and yellow like an insipid yolk of a winter-laid egg, and frosts fell upon frosts, leaving the twigs of bushes encapsuled in cocoons of ice – ice that refused to melt even in the noonday sun. The land had seen other such winters long ago, and these fields had seen sacrifices of capes of feathers, brightly hued cloaks of jay, kingfisher and magpie plumes, that were cast into a fire of apple twigs to persuade the gods to release the sun from the place where it had gone to die; but that had all been long ago, a simple foolishness best forgotten. Men now simply waited for the sun to return. 'A rock age, an iron age, a fire age and an ice age before the world shall end,' the Voluspa singers had chanted when winters like this seized the land.

Lepus' kind had seen many such winters, weathered many such

times, after the melting ice had drowned the retreat to the south, a time when the Ice Age had pondered whether it was time to be done, and hares had survived on lichens and mosses. Those whose constitutions could endure such food survived, and the rest – well, it had always been that way with hares; there was no place for the soft and the weak in a world where all would find hares prey. Thus Lepus, too, would survive, his bowels racked with flux, his faeces fluid and foul through ingesting bad provender. Yet he would survive, existing on what little fat his vital organs had put aside for such an emergency, redigesting that which was almost totally indigestible, finding sustenance on viands the like of which not even a rat could eat. Spring would find his species lean and weak, with coats dull and matted, body fat depleted. But spring would also find the species still abundant – as it always had and might always do. Spring would bring the grasses again, and the sun, but that was a far-away season as yet. 'If Winter comes, can Spring be far behind?' the poet had asked cheerily, but this year the onset of winter would find the spring long overdue, and even modern man might begin to wonder if perhaps the sun had not died. To any it would be a hard winter. To some it would be their last.

The badgers at Cotters End – those who lived in the deep fortress-like citadel undiggable by spade and terrier – slept long, venturing out only rarely during the icy days, their bodies, different from the bodies of other beasts, able to adjust their weight and water content, able to live on their stores of slimy, musky fat. For seven days they remained within the set with no tracks to indicate their presence, and folk began to wonder whether the ancients were right and these ursine, brawling battlers did sleep out the winter. But on the seventh day the boar left the set, ravenous and fearsome, his belly craving food, his flesh no longer content to rely on its own fat reserves. He sniffed at the icy air, tasting the floating ice crystals on his gums, snorted, and began to forage. It was nearly dawn before he found food of any sort. A rabbit, survivor of the harvest massacre, but carrying tiny pieces of lead embedded close to its skinny spine, crippled with cold and suppurating badly, fell prey to the boar, this least nimble of stoats. The badger crunched its tiny emaciated body, snuffing out its scream with grunting and munching and falling upon the near fleshless carcass to eat fur, flesh and bone, leaving nothing but specks of blood and tiny tufts of down. It was a poor meal, but his kind were used to privations, the very foetus deep within his mate's belly developing only in fits and starts, thriving and growing when food was plentiful, dormant when times were hard.

Thus it was a hard time, unkind to birds and beasts and folk, a time of testing the strain, of proving the virtues and strengths of each member of a species, ensuring that only the strong would survive to perpetuate their kind. And then, quite suddenly, the snows went, turning the still-frozen land into an icy quagmire, allowing the grass to grow again and the sun to return to Cotters End.

Spring found Lepus razor-thin, his thigh bones protruding through his fur and his bowels raw with flux. The new grass scoured him somewhat, but his very fibre was alive with a tingling sensation, a wild anxiety he had never before experienced. A new ragged vitality radiated from him, and he was restless and nervy as a newly broken colt. Every nerve in his body seemed to throb with life, and his belly was beset with a hunger food could not assuage. He was already paranoid, aware that any moving thing could mean him harm, but now also became sensitive, aggressive, fearful of even familiar objects, inanimate things he had known since birth. A gatepost on the land midway between Middlemarsh and Cotters End unnerved him, causing him to jack-knife into flight as he passed it and to continue his flight for miles, running himself to a state of exhaustion, pausing, resting, remembering somewhat, and then resuming his wild, insane, panic-stricken flight.

The Old Ones, those concerned with wisdom before man paused to peck at the pseudo-religion called science, said that souls returned to the bodies of beasts with the return of the pale sun, and that the gyrations, the Dervish-like abandonments of hares, were battles between souls, each trying to enter an empty body; but the fever that beset Lepus, the wild frenzy that burned in his loins, was in fact the need to take a mate, his flight a desire to mark out territory against rival males. No longer did the hares of Cotters End gather together to dance the strange eldritch dances of the autumn. Each and every male hare now appeared to him as an aggressor, one who, by defending itself, was attacking him.

He chanced one dawn upon an older jack, rubbing its chin against the bars of the gate that divided Vickery's property from the fields of the Langman estate. The sight of such a mundane gesture drove Lepus to paroxysms of rage, of blind unreasoning fury, and he leaped into the air, twisting like an acrobat. He stalked the male like a somewhat neurotic cat as the older jack watched his approach, equally incensed by some slight mannerism he had seen Lepus perform. They stood nose to nose, quivering with fury, desiring to rip, rend and tear each other to pieces, their minds filled with red mist, oblivious to danger. Then they exploded, leaping at each other like characters in a Chinese soap opera, striking at each other with huge hind legs – blows that could disembowel should the claws strike the soft belly of the adversary. They darted at each other, scraping slivers of fur and skin, their eyes wide with fury, oblivious to pain or approaching danger. For ten or more minutes they fought an outlandish battle, as might be seen in a bad dream: a duel betwixt incongruous, wildly misshapen opponents. But such battles do not proceed unto death, and Lepus soon realized his foe to be older, stronger, more adept in the fighting of hares. Lepus stopped, staring hard at the older buck, panting, his fury abated somewhat. After a moment he avoided the stare of the older jack, and began to browse on some unpalatable weed, chinning the bitter stems, avoiding the glazed stare of the other hare. It was a seemingly aimless gesture, but it was a means of backing down in a fight, a method developed over a million or so years, or maybe a mannerism present in the common stock that spawned all beasts. It was a method of withdrawing from a fight, a way of ensuring that death struggles did not take place, a method of ensuring that the strong and victorious were not too badly maimed to continue to breed the line.

Lepus ambled off to feed nearby, the old jack watching him intently, as intently as only hawks and hares can watch. The old jack would mate a dozen does that year, and his young would be born in twenty or more spots that spring, but Lepus would remain celibate for this season, or practically so, for he would serve an old doe, barren yet still in heat, a wanderer, an itinerant, as are the senile of all species, a doe that would couple with a score of jacks, each one lying cheek to jowl with her and then serving her with furious thrusts. Short sharp love-making sessions characterized her tribe: sessions full of pent-up passions, followed by indifference or an aggression to the doe. A score of suitors would pursue her, court her in the rude fashion of their breed, filling her with their seed, but since she was old the couplings saw no fruit. It was best they did not, for with her increasing age her speed waned and she would not see out that year, ragged and bony as she was from the effects of snow and the persistence of suitors. Four months from now some tinkers, heedless of closed season – as they are of all man-made laws – would course her with a team of dogs slipped untidily, and they would take her, rending her body asunder till her meat was of no use. It was perhaps as well that her body could no longer bear fruit.

The restless, tumultuous times continued well into spring, aimless, wild, unreasoning desires overcoming Lepus daily. 'As mad as a March hare' proverbially described these antics, but it was nearly May before the insanity left his tribe and the males began to feed together again on the meadow-lands. It was a time of danger, these

40

cold days of the March rut, days when winter considered yielding to spring, but yet seemed unsure it was time to do so.

These were times when he was heedless of danger, unbelieving or uncaring that harm could befall him. Yet harm was ever close at hand, danger around every hedge, ever present in each and every field, for tonight he would be destined to meet the most dangerous of his foes. Tonight he would meet the lampers.

'Do you reckon you can sell the sods if we catch them?'

'As many as you can take.'

'Out of season, though. Out of season a month or more,' remarked Lyle.

'Aye, a bit,' said Harris, and continued to comb his greasy hair, gazing into the mirror as he did so to get his 'best side'.

'Does'll be pregnant, milky,' put in Lyle.

'We'll skin them and sell them cleaned, then. No bugger'll know or complain.'

Harris continued to comb his greasy locks. He had enjoyed a narcissistic love affair for some ten years now, and would continue to do so for the rest of his days. Life had not used him badly, for he had left school with no ambitions, writing 'Viceroy of India' for his job choice, and failed at every form of employment attempted. Life was a joke, a ribald prank, played at the state's expense. He had never seriously contemplated work, though he had ventured into various entrepreneurial jaunts, all of which had come unstuck, and one of which had served to ensure that he stayed two more years at the state's expense. It was Harris's lot to be a nearly man: a man nearly educated, nearly employed, nearly criminal, but never really toppling the edges to be labelled. He had been nearly married, and lived at this time with a woman who had also seen better days, but would see considerably worse before her play with Harris was ended.

Lyle was different. He had spent his childhood as a lonely boy, an outcast among his schoolmates, the sort of kid all his fellow school children seem to hate without actually being able to explain why. Lyle had been shunned by his fellows, rejected by the young girls, and had taken to the woods like an uneloquent, unlettered Thoreau. By the age of thirteen he knew most of what there was to know about birds and had become interested in hunting – an interest that consumed him – and though he passed through the period where he slew everything quite quickly, his desire to hunt, the awesome excitement that preceded the catch of any creature from rat to hare, had never left him. Lyle hunted for kicks, lamping and coursing his lurcher at rabbits and hares, sometimes eating his catch but usually giving it away to workmates – gifts that he considered would make him somewhat more popular, for the infant quality that turns all men against another of their kind had stayed with him from childhood into adult life.

When Harris first saw him, he realized the awful loneliness that must beset such a man as Lyle, sensed the proximity of a fast and easy buck as a pig will nose out truffles, and had befriended him. The taking of quarry by artificial lights was new to Harris, but the spirit of the entrepreneur burned strongly in him, and he set about seeking a market for poached coneys and hares. He had failed to find one. Most game merchants merely wished him well and passed him on to another, and no one had been prepared to commit themselves to taking the Eldorado-type hauls he promised. It was, as Lyle had reminded him, the wrong season, but Harris lived in a cocoon of lies and half-truths, an unreal world that even Lyle questioned. After every haul that Lyle made, Harris frantically tried to hawk the rapidly putrefying carcasses of the rabbits around the pubs, finally giving Lyle the money for them out of his own pocket; for to admit that he could not sell them would be to lose face, and someone like Harris must never lose face, not even to an outcast such as Lyle. Harris needed the entrepreneurial image as desperately as Lyle needed company, and hence another venture was being planned, another chance for Harris to try for the crock of gold.

Lyle's lurcher lay in the hearth and yawned. She was a peculiar mixture, lacking height, class or quality. In her veins ran a hotch-potch of Bedlington terrier, whippet, greyhound, collie blood, and a bit else besides. She yawned and stretched. Harris eyed his protégée without comprehending anything of her qualities. Lyle stroked her lovingly.

'There's no moon tonight, Harris, and the wind's picking up. Chances are for a bloody good haul. We could work Cotters End and work back to Ridgeway. It was alive with rabbits along there last season, and the Colonel's got a stock of hares on the other side of the river. We leave the long-eared ones alone and pitch for coneys, I reckon.' His bitch touched his hand with her paw, insisting he stroke her again. 'Take a bloody load tonight, every one alive and unmarked.'

Harris's ears pricked like a fox's. He'd had offers for live rabbits from two villains he'd met at the dog track only a few days before, rabbits designed to speed up a particular dog. Harris was unmoved by the loathsomeness of catching live prey to inspire slavering grey-hounds to greater efforts.

'Yes, take some live ones tonight, Lyle. Don't neck them, then. I can use some live ones to sell.'

Lyle wasn't listening. He seemed more concerned with twisting the

43

fine silky hairs on the beard of his lurcher, an action the bitch found rapturous.

'All right for tonight then, Harris,' he muttered. 'Pick me up here at twelve-thirty. We'll lamp Cotters End. If you can sell them, she'll take them. What'll you do with the live ones?'

But Harris had gone without answering.

That afternoon the breeze began to pick up, bending the trees in Ridgeway Wood, causing the sapling branches to rattle together. Lyle watched the wind build with satisfaction. 'Good 'un, girl, a good 'un,' he whispered to the bitch, who lay supine, lazy like all running dogs when not actually working. By late afternoon, Lyle had souped up his motor-cycle battery and checked his lamp and equipment ready for the night's hunting.

'Slay 'em we will,' he said, ragging the silky top-knot on the lurcher's head. 'Slay 'em,' he muttered. 'Just watch.' And he went to bed for three hours to be ready for the night's activities.

By evening it was almost a gale and the last winds of winter began to lift the tiles on Brennan's cottage, causing them to clatter and clang back into place. It would be a lamper's dream of a night, a high, gusty wind rocking the tree tops, and the night pitch-black: 'Blacker than a mole's arse-hole,' as Lyle described it.

That evening Harris met two teenage girls in the bar and regaled them with his adventures and obvious lies. They listened to him for a while, giggling inanely, and then left the dissipated raconteur to his beer, leaving him for a crowd of rugby-club lads who came through the door. 'Ah well, can't win 'em all,' he murmured to himself, though truth be told it was few he could win, for he had a knack of being able to make the sort of conversation that seemed to repel normal women.

'Shit!' he uttered, feeling his insides heaving with the beer he had drunk. 'Shit! I'm off lamping tonight with Lyle. Don't bloody feel like it, and Christ knows where I'll sell the rabbits. This is a fine mess you've got me into, Stanley,' he mumbled, combing his greasy hair, staring at his reflection in the mirror of the bar.

At one o'clock his van lurched to a halt outside Lyle's house. 'Christ, where you been, where the bloody hell you been?' Lyle spat out. 'Thought you weren't bloody coming.'

'Had a business deal to transact,' lied Harris, remembering the hour he had spent retching behind the wall of the pub.

'Yeah, O.K.,' replied Lyle. 'But the night's bloody nigh gone. You can't piss about when you're lamping, Harris. You've not got all the time in the world, you know.'

'Reckon you'll get any?' said Harris, changing the subject of his tardiness.

'Get any! Hell, the place is bloody alive with rabbits. Bloody alive. Crawling with them. I lamped it last year and took twenty-eight in one evening. Twenty-eight, and that's bloody going it, you know.'

Harris was not listening. He combed his hair wistfully, remembering the blonde teenager he'd tried to seduce so unsuccessfully. 'Christ, I should have stuck at it with her,' he lied to himself. 'A dead eager little bitch if ever I saw one.'

His thoughts returned to Lyle's babblings as the other man trekked on.

'Christ, he's a boring little turd,' Harris almost said aloud as he switched on the van ignition. 'Yes, as boring a little bugger as I'll ever meet.'

The van headed towards Cotters End and the Eldorado hunting grounds of which Lyle had spoken.

They parked in a gateway in the same spot where the two lovers had parked, the self-same lovers who had attempted to run down Lepus in their car. 'Leave the car here and walk,' whispered Lyle. 'It's safest. If the Panda cars see a car here they'll reckon it's a couple "at it".' He chuckled at the inanity of his own joke. ' "At it",' he repeated.

'God, you're a bloody half-wit,' thought Harris. 'No wonder you're lonely, addle-brained sod.' Mentally he stuck the label "boring bugger" on his companion and quickened his stride.

'Keep off the gravel, you're like a bloody Walt Disney horse,' hissed Lyle. 'Every bloody thing'll be back in their holes listening to you.'

Harris tried to silence his footfall, but merely developed an incongruous walk as a result.

In the meadows of Cotters End the branches of ash trees clashed together in the wind and the pastures were brushed with gusts that swept up from the river. Rabbits fed far out from their burrows, confident that the night and its gustiness offered sanctuary. Far out into the meadows Lepus grazed, plucking the fresh stalks of clover aggressively, stopping to stamp and rip at the herbage, for the fury of the March rut, the spring madness, was still with him. He moved from clover patch to clover patch, nibbling at random, for the aggressive spirit that burned within him was not quenched by his browsing. A strong scent of fox wafted across the field towards him, and he froze, scarcely breathing, ears cocked to detect any hint of danger.

There was a shrill yickering scream, a scream that continued for a minute or so as the young dog fox, as celibate and love-maddened as Lepus, chanced upon a young rabbit scarcely twelve feet from the hedgerow. He snapped at the running shape and his teeth met across the loins of the racing rabbit and with paws and fangs he pinned the coney to the earth. He held it for a while, intoxicated with the scent of its fear but lacking purchase enough to kill the struggling, screaming creature. Soon the struggles became less furious and the screams took on a sobbing, pitiful bleat that faded into a falsetto squeal as the rabbit expired, eyes still bulging with fear, legs still thrashing with the spasms of death as if the mind had accepted defeat but the body refused to surrender. A minute later the young male lifted the cadaver, carrying it to a disused burrow under the rhododendron bushes in the Colonel's garden.

The fox had already killed twice that night; first a moorhen grounded by the storm, shaken from the branches of a low tree, and secondly a rat; but he had been dispossessed of his kills by another male, a stronger, older male whose scent had musked the area round Cotters End, and land that is musked is the territory of the male who has musked it. The young dog fox had snarled at the intruder, baring its fangs, hissing like a cat, arching his back and fluffing his tail as he mantled the carcass; but the gesture had not frightened the older male who gently removed both carcasses from the youngster, leaving the young fox spitting furiously, impotent in his rage. Now the youngster would feed on the coney in the sanctuary of the old burrow, noisily chomping the meat, swallowing flesh and fur. His would be a celibate year and all his courtships fruitless.

Lepus when he heard the scream became as tense as a bow-string, but the yickering sensation of the screams calmed him somewhat, for some innate knowledge that the predator would offer no further danger now that his belly was full is ever present in the meek, allowing them to live out their days in relative tranquillity. The dog fox would do no further hunting that night, indulge in no further killing. Man alone, the eternal predator, will set out upon a hunt with his belly full – man, the arch-predator, the wilful butcher of all species, his own included, seemingly determined to ensure that only his kind shall inherit the planet's surface. Thus man alone was to be always feared, always kept in awe, not because beasts would sense his superiority but because only man is capricious in his killing, slaying at a whim rather than from need, erratic in his instinctive behaviour, wasteful in his destruction. Lepus was destined to come to know this twisted predatory urge better before dawn rose over the fields of Cotters End.

'Careful with that gate,' Lyle nagged. 'Quiet as possible. Jesus,

46

you're like a bloody pit pony.'

Harris stifled back any rejoinder.

'Quiet now, quiet.' Lyle continued his advice like a mother advising her teenage daughter on how to behave at her first party.

They stepped slowly into the field, their footfalls muffled by the sound of the wind. A lark rising from the grass startled Harris and he turned to run. Lyle grabbed him. 'Fine bloody poacher. For all your talk of being a hard case, a bloody bird puts you to flight. You're like a sick tart.'

Lyle had become a different person. In the town – Harris's domain – Lyle was ill at ease, easily cowed by Harris's bombastic attitude, suffering the boasts and lies in silence; but here, in the dark fastness of Cotters End, he was in his element and his skills would ensure they would finish the night full-handed and uncaught. 'In!' he slapped his side gently, and the lurcher bitch and Harris slid fluidly to heel. 'Watch now, Harris. Wits about you now. Watch!'

He flicked on the beam of the lamp he was carrying and shone the brilliant white light around the field. The night was alive with the ruby eyes of rabbits, ears held close to their backs to escape detection. 'What did I tell you, Harris? Don't lie do I, mate?' Lyle whispered triumphantly.

They walked up to the nearest feeding coney, moving slowly, fox-like in their stealth, the lurcher bitch aquiver with excitement while the rabbit crouched in the forlorn hope of escaping detection. Forty, thirty yards, and suddenly the rabbit took flight, moving like an arrow towards its burrow. The shadowy shape of the lurcher suddenly propelled itself forward and snapped up the rabbit with the dexterity of a cricketer fielding a cricket ball, retrieving the live and squealing animal to Lyle's outstretched hand.

'See what I mean? Best there is, isn't she?' All Lyle's geese were swans. 'Don't lie, do I?'

'Keep it live, Lyle, I want some live, don't forget.'

'O.K., clever sod, you carry a dozen bleeding live rabbits around all night.'

Lyle twisted the neck of the squealing rabbit, moving the head to an almost unbelievable angle as the squealing ceased suddenly, though the carcass continued to convulse, voiding dung and urine. 'Carry it, Harris,' said Lyle to his now somewhat subservient partner.

Another, another and another rabbit squeaked its way to death, each retrieved to hand, each slain with the dextrous, pitiless, efficient twist of the neck. The eyes of the carcasses became dull and the bodies, carried by Harris, ceased to twitch and shudder. 'You always get a record haul here, Harris. I told you.'

The excitement of the first kills had begun to wane and Harris became suddenly irritated by his colleague's whispered boasts. 'God, you're a boring sod, a bloody know-all at heart. How in hell do you expect me to sell this bloody mound of rabbits you're expecting to catch,' he thought. The weight of rabbits seemed to increase at every step.

The beam touched Lepus, illuminating him clearly, and with ears erect, eyes bulging, he prepared for flight.

Lyle flicked off the beam. 'Hare. Let the bugger go. It'll knacker the dog and chances are you won't be able to sell the sod even if you sell the rabbits.'

Darkness bathed Lepus once more, but he stood erect, ready for flight, not moving, hoping the canopy of darkness would hide him from the hunters.

'Won't that dog take a hare then? Not fast enough is she?' chided Harris.

'She's taken a stack. I'm just saying there's no point running a hare if it's rabbits you're lamping. A hare'll bugger a dog for the rest of the night.'

'Not up to it, is that it?' sneered Harris, eager to take revenge on the now over-cocky Lyle.

'Told you, Harris. Hare'll bugger the dog,' replied Lyle angrily.

'Not up to it? You don't want to show her up?' Harris still questioned.

'O.K., smart bugger, watch this.' And once again the brilliant white light bathed the alert form of Lepus.

He stood carved in stone, his heaving flanks clearly visible in the beam. Yet he remained still, still hoping to escape detection. Nearer still came the dog and Lepus began to move – not rapidly, for a wall of blackness encompassed him. Then the hot scent of the dog gave him an indication that death was close and he began to run, desperate to find the sanctuary the walls of darkness offered; but, try as he might, the blinding light, a narrow corridor of day in the fields of darkness, continued to shine on him. He jinked and became invisible, but the whiteness found him again. Suddenly, out of the blackness, the dog struck at him, the teeth scoring his skin, and he rolled to escape capture, bowling into the blackness again. But there was no sanctuary, little respite, for the beam illuminated him again. Again she struck and again he rode the blow, weaving, bobbing, ducking, rolling, frantic to escape the whiteness and the ever-eager fangs of the dog.

These were his fields, his domain, yet they seemed unfamiliar to him now. He turned to the hedge, for the hedge was pock-marked with escape holes, but again the beam brought him back. He turned near the hollow in the centre of the field, twisting, turning to escape the dog, running aimlessly, madly now, still following the silent instructions given out by the corridor of light. In daylight he would have made the dog look an idiot, but it was not daylight except within the narrow confines of the beam. The dog struck him again and he squealed, a piteous squeal, a cry resembling the bleat of a stricken soul, and Lyle, now exuberant, almost shouted, 'Hear that, Harris? Who said she's not up to it. She damn nigh had the sod over that time.'

Lepus balked at the hedge again, turning back into the field, and swung in a semi-circle back towards the hollow, but the dog, not confined within the corridor of light, sensed the arc that the hare was running and struck across the semi-circle to turn him off the hedge again. Panic now seized Lepus, panic that lent further speed to his already furiously moving legs, and for a brief moment he outstripped the dog. Yet there was still no peace for him, for again the dog gained, remorseless as the hound of hell itself. The lurcher closed with him again, and the hot fear-scent emitting from the hare's furiously working body seemed to give her fading strength reason to continue. He weaved out of the beam, but again the whiteness found him.

'Christ, how the little bastard goes,' muttered Harris, suddenly appreciative of Lepus' speed. 'Jesus, just look at him go.'

'Bitch'll get him though,' muttered Lyle breathlessly, mentally running each step with the dog. 'She'll get the bugger.'

For a second Lepus went out of the beam, a brief second, scarcely time for a heart to miss a beat, but again the light found him and again the dog struck.

He was frightened now, badly frightened, more terrified than ever before in his brief terror-filled life. There was nothing he could do to evade the strikes of the dog and the phantom moonlight of the beam. Furthermore, his strength was beginning to wane and his breath came in fiery gasps punctuated by squeals, as fear overrode discretion. Hedges he had known well were alien to him now in the eerie moonlight of the lamp. Familiar spots became death-traps and, horror of horrors, he seemed no longer to be able to judge distance. He quickened his speed, reduced it, jinked, turned to throw off the pursuing dog, but somehow seemed to be drawn inexorably into the centre of the field, far from the hedge where he could lose the dog and evade the all-searching light. He leaped sideways to avoid the under-

49

strike of the dog, a blow that would have finished him, crushed his spine, torn his body badly, and in leaping went temporarily out of the beam. But the light found him again in a split second. His arc of running had increased, and he was off his normal runs. He turned into the wall of darkness again, and the shock of icy water jarred his body like a collision with a heavy object. He began to swim frantically, incongruously, splashing, floundering, a creature well designed for life on land but ill-at-ease in water. He swam on, and the dog on the bank let loose a yicker.

'Christ, he's buggered the dog. Look there, the sod's blown her. The little bastard's knackered my lurcher.' Lyle began to hurl stones at the swimming hare. The dog stood on the bank, tongue hanging from her mouth, jaws slavering, sides heaving, breath coming erratically.

Lepus gained the far bank, still illuminated by the beam, still pursued by the all-searching light. He shook himself to rid his wet and steaming body of water and mud. He paused a moment, panting with the shock of submersion and the awful efforts of the exertion. His ears were held limply making him look more like a comical toy hare than a real live beast. He shook his coat again and ambled off over the rise and out of the beam. He was safe now, but safety is always a temporary thing for a hare, for like the biblical Son of Man he has no place to hide his head. He was on to new territory now, and that which is new is hostile. He would have little time in which to learn the ways of this land, however, for this bank too held its predators, some more fearsome than those of the bank he had left behind.

Vogel sat upon Kemp's fist and tightened her grip on the glove. With reptilian looks she watched for the movements of Kemp's other hand, eager for the sliver of bloody flesh it held, for, despite her regal demeanour, she was a slave to her belly. 'Our army marches on its stomach,' a Corsican corporal called Bonaparte had said, but Vogel, Vogel was enslaved by her appetite, bound to Kemp with chains forged by hunger. She would do his bidding, heed his call, return obedient to him only because the gnawing pangs of hunger racked her stomach. Vogel was a German word, meaning simply 'bird' – but to call such a creature Vogel was like calling a hurricane a wind. Vogel was more than a bird or, to judge by her flat saurian head and wild paranoid eyes, less than a bird – it was difficult to tell. She gripped the glove still tighter and followed every movement of Kemp's hand.

Slave she was to her belly, but like Paul of Tarsus she had been born free. Her sire had courted her dam in the pine forests of Finland, and a gentle, delicate courtship it had been. He was smaller than her by a third and was careful of her violent, fractious ways. That spring he had courted the female, amorous as a lizard, stilted and careful in his loving, and she had conceived and laid her blood-dappled eggs in a nest that once housed crows and jays. She had brooded long over her eggs, mantling the nest like a contented hen, and only her mad, rage-filled eyes had told her true disposition. She had sat her clutch while the male, obedient to the ways of custom, forged over an aeon of time, had fed her delicate morsels of thrush, speckle-breasted and still twitching and quivering with life. He had fed her in a delicate, restrained manner, mindful perhaps of her unruly disposition, her size and her furious temper – a temper that might make her a widow in moments. Thus he offered his grisly love tokens carefully. It was always the way of goshawks. It was a good way.

She sat her eggs tightly, a harpy among birds, until the eggs chipped and young downy rocs emerged, small but fiercer and more primordial than the birds of Sinbad. Each chick she fed upon the flesh of thrushes and summer birds torn to bloody strips to satiate her screaming, squawking brood, but there is no room in a nest for several feathered banshees, and each chick cast covetous eyes on its fellows, seeing them as food rather than siblings. Vogel was the first hatched and was the strongest. Vogel survived, growing strong on the flesh of her nest-mates. It was always the way with goshawks. It was a good way.

Thus her furious life would have continued and she would have lived to tyrannize and terrify the dwellers in that Finnish pinewood had not fate been perhaps a little unkind. During her third week, when she was peering from her nest like a feathered dragon with vertical umber chest marks, a man had come nailing spikes in the trees, and he had climbed, heedless of the impotent attacks of her sire and dam, and taken her screeching, spitting and screaming in a hamper lined with sacking. She had then lain fearful within a cage, striking at the hands that touched her, erupting into paroxysms of rage whenever the lid of the hamper was opened. Kemp had bought her, taking delight in her strength and fury, finding pleasure in dominating such a mass of seething resentment and ferocity. But it was Kemp's way to find pleasure in such things. Kemp knew much of the ways of predators. He was one himself.

The Hippocratic oath that Kemp had taken as a doctor did not extend to beasts. He took delight in hunting, pleasure in killing, in spite of his thriving medical practice. His needs were modest and he found pleasure only in carnage. He was a small, unlovely man, 'dapper', one of the village women had called him; and his wife, a small, tasteful, bland woman, had conceived two daughters out of obedience rather than love because Kemp had thought it proper that a doctor should have children. There was a strange iciness about Kemp's manner, an iciness that seemed to melt only on the demise of some bird or beast. His colleagues referred to him jokingly as an atavism, a throw-back to a more shadowy time in the history of man, but it was not so. Kemp in no way resembled the hunter who had moved north from an African Eden following the food herds. Kemp was an anachronism, but he was perhaps a precursor of things to come rather than a throw-back to a more distant past. *Homo novus* would have classified Kemp, a new type of man prepared to see the earth leeched of its species. He was in no way sympathetic to the beasts he hunted, treating death with a hearty indifference. His kind was not new to the human race, however. Several of his sub-species had caused the extinction of the auk, the dodo and the Irish elk. He should have been sympathetic to Vogel and her furious, predatory nature. They had much in common.

So the pair had come together and their lives and ways interlaced, for no man, not even Kemp, can train a goshawk without it becoming his thoughts in waking and sleeping. 'Woe to him who knows the mystery of the rivers,' some long forgotten poet had said. 'For he shall know no wife nor child, no horse nor hound.'

Slowly, with infinite slowness, the pair had welded into a team, fused into the super-predator, a creature with the pitiless intelligence of Kemp and the speed and slaying power of Vogel; but the binding of the two, the symbiosis, had not been easy. Vogel hated man with a hatred born of a thousand years of persecution, an archetypal hatred of the species that had captured, starved and trained her kind. Then, as the sport of falconry had fallen from favour, men had slain the goshawk as it preyed, and preyed too successfully, at that, on the game birds on which man himself delighted in preying. Thus the biter was bitten and the slayer slain. 'The Angel of Death came and slaughtered the slaughterer,' Brennan would have said, but Kemp was not Brennan and had little use for poetry or its accompanying softness of soul.

So the duel between Vogel and Kemp had begun, a duel that would know only one victor. Vogel had been fed well on hens freshly killed, still fluttering, tossed into her in the darkness of the room Kemp called a mews. She had stood there, watching the death contortions of the hens, hungry, famished, but fearing to feed while the shadows cast by Kemp's lamp made commonplace objects terrifying. At first she had bated to escape those flickering shadows and fed only after the mews became silent and dark again. Vogel had gorged on the red and bloody meat, ripping the still-warm flesh to slivers, devouring flesh, bone and feather, gorging until her crop was bloated, and then waiting in the darkness until another luckless bird or beast was thrown to her; but the time of gorging was drawing to a close, the seven fat weeks were about to become seven lean ones. She was grown now, and her feathers perfect, her bones and muscles stronger than they would have been had she remained in her Finnish homeland, for Kemp had fed her well; but the warm days, the times when her belly would always be full and her temper always fractious, were drawing to an end. It was time for Kemp to take her up for training.

Screaming, clawing, bating, next day she had been jessed with straps of leather – leather tanned in Spain from the skins of dogs, for Kemp was macabre in all things, and wearing these fetters she had sat on Kemp's fist, panting, furious, hating mankind with a loathing that only captive wild creatures can experience. She had bated from that hated fist a hundred, no a thousand times, as Kemp had walked her, and each time as a temper tantrum had caused her to erupt into paroxysms of fury, so Kemp had tenderly lifted her back to the fist. Thus she began to accept the fist as a perch, and though she bated often and furiously, the bates became less furious and less frequent as time went on. Still she refused meat from Kemp's hand and daily her weight dropped. Soon she became ravenous and her belly filled with bitter juices that gnawed at the stomach linings, bubbling within her, causing her desire for food to become intense. Then she began to notice and peck at the slivers of raw and bloody meat that Kemp offered. One day she pecked at the bloody morsel offered her and tore fine shreds of the meat, gobbling it quickly lest the offering disappear. Kemp smiled coldly at the feeding Fury. It was time now to progress with her education. He had starved her into submission. Now he would wake her.

He entered her mews early next day, and she, tethered by her jesses to her perch of wood and sacking, bated away from the slowly moving man. He caught her up gently, uttering soothing words to her, assuring the screaming, clawing maniac that she was a delight. Attila had said the same of the goshawk, but it was a curious type of man who would agree with the King of the Huns. Still Kemp had caught her up, and now he would carry her, carry her until she reeled with exhaustion and slept upon his fist; but that would be some time hence, for now she would 'bate and beat and would not be obedient' throughout the time of the carrying. Kemp carried her all that day, his arm aching with the strain, his face and head buffeted with the beating of the wings, and each time she bated he would move his hands slightly and flick her back on the fist. Slowly, with infinite slowness, the bating became less frequent and her wing beats and flailings weaker. As the day passed she had stood upon his fist, weary, exhausted, sleep-shotten, but furiously resisting the sensation overcoming her making her sway drunkenly upon the gauntlet. A dozen times she began to nod, but Kemp always gently shook her back to wakefulness.

By midnight she was swooning with exhaustion, and still Kemp carried her. Gradually her eyelids began to close and she permitted Kemp to stroke her beak, to touch her umber-streaked breast and even to place her head beneath her wing. Vogel slept, stirring in her sleep like a fitful Kraken. Kemp smiled. This waking had been an unnecessary gesture, a pointless duel, a method practised only by falconers of old, but now rarely used to school a hawk. To Kemp it was necessary to master a hawk, as he had mastered and broken his wife's spirit and his daughters' enthusiasm for life. Kemp needed mastery over beasts. 'And God gave man dominion over all animals,' Genesis had said, but Kemp needed to experience this dominion, needed to experience excitement from such mastery. Thus Vogel, defiant and formidable, was made docile. He would starve her further now to make her more obedient.

Kemp began to keep her fine now: 'sharp set', the ancients called it, hungry to the point where her only thoughts were those of food, and

55

she became too famished to bate away when he approached her perch in the darkened mews. Her eyes became more insane, the insanity produced by hunger rather than fear. Her weight was dropping daily and her vital organs becoming depleted of fat. Kemp fed her sparingly, encouraging her to jump to the fist to be fed, encouraging her to leap to the fist or else go to bed hungry. When she was stubborn, obstinate, reluctant to come to the glove, he soaked her victuals in water, wringing out the flesh, squeezing the life-giving juices from the meat and giving her the whitened, nourishment-lacking food. It filled her belly but had no virtue, and next day she was empty and craving. She would leap now ten feet or more to the fist, obedient to the hand that held the morsels of meat, a slave to Kemp and his bagful of slivers of beasts; and still he required her to leap still further for the tiny gobbets of flesh he proffered. Twenty, thirty feet she would leap, and then, one day, Kemp took his ravenous bird and fed her tiny portions of well-washed meat, meat mostly white, colourless fibre rather than flesh.

Next day she knew hunger like she had never known, and she paced upon the perch, moving her feet restlessly, waiting for Kemp to come to the mews. It was on this day that she was flown free of the twine that bound her. She had the choice of freedom now, but her mind, her every fibre, was geared only to the redness Kemp took from his bag. She flew fast and true, hitting his fist with a smack, poking his hand for the meat, more like a docile parrot than a hawk. Kemp had tamed her. Esau had sold his birthright for a mess of pottage – Vogel had traded liberty for a morsel of meat; but freedom and her forest life meant little to her now. All that was important to her was that she should slake her burning hunger on the scraps of meat offered her.

Kemp had given her a watery smile and continued with her training. She had been subdued by weariness, made tame by hunger, and now she would be allowed to practise the sole art for which the Almighty had created this stupid, rage-filled, reptilian monster. She would be taught to kill, and her teaching would delight a Gille de Rais. Kemp persuaded some youths to catch him some diminutive rabbits by ferreting and netting. These he took live and pressed into the talons of the baffled Vogel.

The first diminutive bunny had remained motionless, its muscles rigid with terror beneath those scimitar-like talons. For a while, Vogel had eyed the rabbit curiously, baffled at the furry bundle of bone and casting Kemp had given her. She had prodded it with her beak, encouraging it to move perhaps, but it had merely closed its eyes and become more inert. Perhaps it was the beating of that frightened heart that awoke the spirit of fury within Vogel, or maybe a tiny flicker of a tense muscle had indicated life, for suddenly those sword-like talons had tightened on the rabbit and its scream choked in its throat as the inexorable grip forced the life from the tiny body. At the death of the rabbit, Vogel had come alive. She had driven her talons into the furry creature, exhilarated by the muscle spasms of the dying beast. Kemp had allowed her to mantle her prey, to threaten him with a lizard-like hiss, and to peck a morsel or so of flesh. Kemp watched her and allowed her to savour her moment of triumph. It was good she should do so.

Next day she was cast off at a live rabbit, a rabbit allowed to run a little, though it was little it could run, tethered as it was to a heavy stick attached to its back legs. Still, its jerky, pathetic movements had excited her to fury, and she had left the fist to crash headlong into the tiny tethered rabbit, some long-forgotten instinct making her grip the struggling, screaming animal by the head and loins. Slowly its threshings and screaming had become weaker and its head had ceased to give those pitiful puppet-like jerks. Vogel had dined on the rabbit, but she was never allowed to fly another coney again. Vogel had been brought from that Finnish forest to be trained to fly hare. There were many falconers who boasted they had goshawks who would fly and take a hare, but Vogel would do so in truth.

Lepus fed well that night, and the daylight found him still nibbling the second crop of grass that had grown now the hay was cut. It had been an uneasy season, and he had taken time to learn the labyrinth of hedgerows and fences on the Colonel's estate. It was a new land, an unfamiliar land, but it was a land he must learn if he was to survive. Draycott's Bridge, a stone-built structure constructed by an enthusiastic supporter of Telford who had built it a century ago, separated Lepus from his home fields, but it might have been a star's distance away. Draycott's Bridge had always separated Cotters End from Dowley, a territorial boundary observed by man and beast alike.

It was the time of hunting again now, and some primeval instinct was at work within the hare, making him more tense, quicker in thought and action, than he had been during the drowsy summer in Dowley. It had been a time of calm in the wet, warm summer, and he had grown somewhat indifferent to danger during this lotus time. Twice he had been harassed by louts with lurchers who had slipped their small pack of dogs on him, dogs that collided in flight, dogs that fought each other rather than pursued him in deadly earnest. He had not exerted himself a great deal in trying to avoid them, for he was now aware of the measure of such beasts, and as they had gained on him, snarling and baying at the proximity of the kill, he had slipped into the high barley through paths that he and his kind had run repeatedly. For a while the louts had hunted the barley, trampling down its ripening stalks, creating havoc but failing to find him; it troubled him little, for danger and death are constant companions to a creature such as Lepus. For a while he had lain up in the deepest part of the corn, crouching, ears back, unobserved in the yellowing barley, but after a while he forgot his fear and cat-napped, one eye always open to detect impending danger.

Danger was ever present. A dozen times or more he had been stalked by foxes, who had circled the napping hare, their bellies to the ground, their hind quarters trembling with anticipation. During the early summer he had repeatedly run foul of a vixen and her cubs – the vixen an ancient grey fox brought in from Wales to improve the existing inbred fox population. She had been old when taken, dug by some lads with terriers and spades, and she had been as lean as all hill foxes who live on voles and mice. The vixen had been turned loose near Dowley House and had thrived on the fat lands and good hunting of the shires, growing leisurely in her old age. Thus she had been served by a young dog fox that spring, and had borne him a litter of cubs, but the fat living, the leisurely hunts for rabbits and the gleanings from midden piles, had made her apathetic. For six years she had outrun the hill packs of Wales, fought off the terriers in the deep crevice-like earths of Merioneth, but she would not survive the first hunt of the season in Dowley, and she would be pulled down screaming like a cat by callow unentered hounds out cubbing.

Twice Lepus had nearly been taken by the collie at the Big House, a dog lacking in speed but strong in wisdom. He had watched Lepus turn to the corn to evade him a hundred or so times during the season, and now no longer ran the fleeing hare, but cut across the fields to the barley where he knew Lepus would run. On the second attempt at such chess play he had bowled Lepus, who had rolled beneath the snapping, snarling dog to avoid the bite; but the teeth had connected on his hind legs, and though he lost the dog in the dusty, pollen-filled field of barley, he had lain up sore and bruised after the chase. After this he became as wary of slow, slinking dogs as he had become wary of the fleet and silent hounds who pursued him at Cotters End. Dogs were always adversaries to him, it would always be so, but now the corn was down and the tangled thickets were becoming bare as the chill breeze of autumn swept the fields. Still he had survived all manner of dangers, outrun all his predators. Today, however, it would be a different sort of encounter.

At the surgery house Kemp turned his sherry glass pensively, watching its blurred stickiness reflecting the sporting prints on the wall behind him. He stretched slightly and yawned. Two hours previously he had gone to inspect Vogel, but, though she did not bate away from him as he approached, she was not eager to be picked up, and her talons did not grip his gauntlet with the usual enthusiasm. He decided to wait two hours before flying her; then she would be ready for the hunt, for her belly would indeed be empty, and she would fly with enthusiasm at any quarry. *Yarak*, the Turks called such a condition: a judicious blend of hunger, alertness and deadly earnestness, a time when she would be hungry but not too weak to fly. Four years Kemp had flown Vogel, and he knew the subtle alchemy of her make-up. Two hours and she would be ready. 'Two hours to kill,' he thought, smiling wryly at his own acetic humour.

Two hours later, Vogel was eagerly awaiting her master's return to the mews, frantically pacing the padded perch as far as her leash would let her. She was hungry now, and all traces of indifference had vanished. As the door of the mews opened, she bated towards Kemp and jumped eagerly to his glove, her talons resounding as she struck the hard leather of the gauntlet. The needle-like talons constricted on the glove, and Kemp could feel their power, even through the heavy leather. He stroked her streaked breast, the streaking now horizontal since she had moulted her juvenile plumage, and spoke to her. 'Well, sweeting, the first flight of the season. *Yarak*,' he murmured as he felt the grip tighten and watched her insane scarlet eyes.

Kemp left the mews and walked towards the house with neat measured strides. 'Here, Max,' he called. 'Here,' and his German shorthead pointer strode towards him, head down, swaying as it moved. Vogel bated away from the dog; she had always done so during the early part of a hunt, but before the end of each day she would regard the dappled dog as her ally. Together they set off towards Draycott's Bridge and the meadows beyond, Vogel bating at each and every beast and Max chuntering slightly as he walked. Kemp paused at the first gate after the bridge, opened it, and, like three Apocalyptic horsemen, the trio entered the field, Max casting eagerly, drinking up the scent evaporating from the dew. Twice he stiffened into a half-point, half considering freezing to immobility, but twice two larks rose into the air, their scent gamey as a pheasant.

'Max,' Kemp chided gently, and his words stung the sensitive dog. Max had been bought as a puppy and sired by a German import, and he had only known Kemp. Over the years he had blended with the tiny, emotionless man until he became part of him, a branch of a tree, in fact. He was aware of Kemp's icy disposition, aware of the fact that Kemp found displeasure in the fawning of the dog. Thus the beast became remote, much given to slinking away when approached by strangers.

'Max,' Kemp said piercingly above the jangle of the bells as Vogel bated towards the rising larks. The hound-like dog slunk back behind the man and they began to walk towards Wayland's Covert, a spinney of birch and alder, much overgrown and a sanctuary for fox and pheasant alike. It was an ancient wood – a wood where smiths tempered Saxon swords and carved runes upon the blades, runes which ensured the blades would not bend in battle, or snap, when they struck the chain mail and wooden shields of a foe. Woden's Covert it had once been called, for Woden was the god of smiths, but men forgot the old gods and the names changed: Woden became Wayland, and the wood no longer rang with the clang of metal on anvil and the sibilant hiss of bellows and quenched iron. Now birds perched where the swords of warriors had been forged.

Max halted at Wayland's Covert and posed, rigid as rock. A pheasant ran from a clump of thistles towards the patch of alder. It ran quickly, dragging its left wing slightly, fluttering a few paces but unable to fly. A few days ago it had received a few pellets during the first shoot of the season, pellets that had crippled it, incapacitated it, making it able to run rather than fly, but it would have little time to perfect its newly discovered skills. In three days time a stoat, full-bellied but hunting for pleasure, would chance on the bird, pursuing it through the grass and slaying it with a bite to the skull, hanging on to the threshing, thrashing body until the fluttering ceased, nibbling a mere piece or so as a token gesture, and then leaving the gaudy, iridescent bird to the crows. Now the bird dashed towards the alder bed, uttering its guttural alarm cry as it ran. Max started after it, but the soft-spoken voice of Kemp checked him in mid-flight. Again he slunk back to heel, glancing up at Vogel who was bating furiously at the fleeing cripple. Kemp restrained her, lifting her back to the fist. 'Peace. Peace, my beauty, not yet, not yet awhile.'

Vogel sat there panting, eyes ablaze. Her stomach was almost crying out for bloody nourishment and her mind filled with a red haze of macerated flesh, an orgy of blood, bowels and red ruin. Kemp looked up lovingly – as lovingly as his expressionless face could look. She was ready now, ready to make a bid at the strongest hare, ready to ride it to its death, to pin it 'twixt her razor talons, holding it long enough for Kemp to dispatch it with his knife, stabbing upwards into the throat through the eggshell skull so that the screaming beast's eyes nearly popped from its head through a hybrid between fear and the pressure of the blade.

'On now, Max,' Kemp urged, encouraging the skulking, almost tailless dog to hunt the lower pastures away from Wayland's Covert. The dog ambled forward, swinging its pendulous ears, stump tail protruding at a horizontal angle. He paused awhile, mulling over the sweet and sour scent of Lepus' dung, fresh waste that still held the almost pungent odour. Vogel watched as only a hawk can watch, her entire mind centred on the dog moving rhythmically into the centre of the field, nose down, backside sticking out almost obscenely. Vogel watched, oblivious to all things other than the dog – the dog that was hunting to produce prey for her. Max paused again at a patch of fresh scent, a spot where only an hour ago Lepus had passed a pool of oily-brown urine. Far out into the field Lepus browsed, aware of the trio of hunters. He fed nervously, plucking at the grass, a weather eye open for danger. He would not have long to wait.

Max quickened his pace, his travesty of a tail wagging furiously.

He quartered the ground almost madly now, aware that the quarry was only moments away. The ground reeked of scent, the hot pungent scent of hare. On Kemp's glove Vogel's grip tightened, leaving Kemp's hand sore in spite of the heavy gauntlet that protected the fist from those spiked, crushing claws. Max paused at some thistles, near which Lepus had chinned some broken stalks of ragwort; and then, quite suddenly, Max saw the hare as he sat watching the speckled dog hunting his scent.

Max froze to a point, as immobile and lifeless as a statue by Milo, his back and head forming a straight line, paw half raised, muzzle towards Lepus, tail away. He stood like a huge, ungainly weather-vane as if hypnotized by the hare. Lepus continued to browse as the dog began an effort-filled, slow-motion, exaggerated walk towards him. Lepus had seen such dogs, watched them get near to him, anticipated their sudden dash, matched it with superior speed and then outpaced the beast, out-classed it and out-thought it. There was no need for real anxiety while he could watch the stalking dog, no need for flight yet. Max's every movement, his ridiculous pretence at a stalk, left him in no doubt that he could defeat this quaint and curious-looking animal. He continued to pluck grass more excitedly now, but with only half a glance at the dog. So intent was he on the stalking dog, however, that he failed to notice that Kemp was also stalking him, bird on fist, Vogel furious to be released at the hare. The triangle formed by the dog, the austringer and the feeding hare continued to decrease in size. Lepus became uneasy. There was something wrong here – something out of place, something that perplexed him. He anticipated a sudden short, sharp dash from the dog, but was increasingly aware of Kemp slowly outflanking him. He stretched his limbs ready for flight. It was then that Kemp flung Vogel at him.

Vogel bated and the sound of bells filled the air. He was belled beneath the tail, for he needed those talons to murder, and blood and fur would clog those tinny bells, making them silent. A decade ago the bells had been forged in a dusty workshop in Lahore, fashioned from an alloy of copper, an alloy so thick with dust and dross that no scientist could duplicate the mix. They rang out shrilly in the frosty morning air, one an octave above the other, and through them Lepus first became aware of the danger that crouched upon Kemp's fist. She bated towards Lepus' fleeing form, and Kemp in flinging her off had given her speed an extra boost through a sharp movement of the fist. Lepus crashed into full flight, his hind feet drumming the ground, but Vogel was on him.

She beat across the field after him, an effortless, deceptively slow beat, that looked so leisurely until one saw it eat up all distance between hawk and quarry. *Rameur*, the ancients called the goshawk – 'the rower' – and with rowers' strokes she bore down on the racing hare.

She struck at him almost carefully at first, rising slightly in the air, and fell upon him in a jangle of bells and a flash of talons. He rolled to avoid the aerial attack, bowling clear of the hooks that tore the fur of his rump, bringing a trickle of blood and tufts of wool. But then he was up again, riding the impact of the blow, racing off towards the thicket of Wayland's Covert. Again Vogel rounded on him, her bells nearly screaming as she put in the final plunge at the running hare. He was over now, and she almost held him as he screamed and struggled, evacuating his bladder and bowels, filling the air with stink; but, with a huge effort, he was up again, flanks badly punctured, bleeding from a dozen needle wounds. She swung off to the left, and then came in at him in deadly earnest, footing him in the head causing him to buck like a rodeo horse. Again he slipped, again he evaded those talons that could have held him down, held him so that Kemp could come up on him and finish him with the knife.

He rose again and kicked her off, kicked her with those huge hind legs, raining blows on her that would have deterred any normal hawk. Once more she rose, rolling into the attack, buffeting him, frantic to grip his head and loins, a grip that would hold him and make those formidable kicks impotent; but she missed her footing, snatched at him, ripping his ear from base to tip, causing blood to pour from the wound. He was running now aimlessly, wildly, fearfully, for there was no place in which he could find safety. Dogs he had learned to outpace, learned to outflank, but this stupid reptilian creature, this winged lizard, bore down on him unceasingly. He was small for a jack, Brennan had said, yet with that lack of size had come a speed and agility that put most dogs to shame. But being small he lacked the strength to kick off this winged Fury. Had he been a giant like the jack that lived in the meadows of the Big House – a twelve-pound ponderous beast – he could have kicked off his foe, but he weighed seven pounds or less and his speed and agility could avail him nothing against Vogel. Again she rose, gaining height slightly, rolling into the attack again. *Kampfflunz* – 'battle flight' – the Germans called this roll.

He ducked and jinked to avoid the attack, but quick as he was, she was faster, and the sight of his bloody ears and raw, torn rump made her attack more furious. He bowled, but as he rose she took him with a measured footing, one talon on his head, her hooked cleavers nearly rupturing an eye, and the other across the loins, gripping tightly, claws nearly puncturing the throbbing vicera. Lepus thrashed upon the ground a little, trying to rise, but her mighty grip and the flailing wings and clanging bells drove him back while his eyes bulged in terror. Again he tried to rise, but was borne earthwards again, his body experiencing a sudden weariness, a strange, inexplicable torpor. He tried to rise now, but the strength had left his limbs and he no longer writhed and contorted under those talons. Kemp walked forward slowly, a smile creasing his tiny mouth.

Perhaps the strength had returned to Lepus' weary and sore limbs, perhaps the sight of Kemp and the dog approaching caused him to panic, fear giving back strength to his numbed body. He rose slightly, causing Vogel to release her hold on his head, and then careered off, the hawk gripping his spiked and bloody rump, riding him as a rough-rider rides an unbroken mount. She no longer rose above him now, trying to swoop in to pin him to the ground, but merely hung on to his red and tender hind-quarters, beating her wings to brake, to slow him down while he, desperate to be rid of this demoniac old man of the sea, lashed and kicked at her. She bowled him again and he rolled to avoid the talon that sought his eyes. Then, suddenly, he came upon a drain entrance and slipped inside.

Vogel sat there quizzically, her stupid, blood-clouded brain unable to understand how her prey could have vanished from sight. She sat there, panting and hissing, furious at the miss, her muscles aching with the strain of the hunt, her belly screaming out for the meat so nearly hers.

Kemp approached and she jumped to his fist for the morsel he proffered. 'Check it, Max,' he murmured, and Max stuck his pink and blotched nose down the drain and snorted excitedly. 'He's in there, Vogel, my love, my sweeting, and rightly yours. By all the powers that be you shall have him too.' He peered up the drain to where Lepus lay panting, dripping from a score of deep punctures and slashes. 'He's yours, Vogel, I promise,' Kemp hissed, and he took two large stones and blocked the end of the drain. 'Tomorrow we'll flush him, my sweeting. Tomorrow you shall take him, I promise,' he murmured as the hawk gulped down the shreds of flesh that Kemp took from his falconer's bag. 'Eat lightly, my sweeting, so that tomorrow you will be sharp enough to appreciate a meal of hare. Tomorrow, Vogel, tomorrow I promise you shall feed on him.'

Lamia paced restlessly within her hutch, peering through the bars. Lamia – it was seemingly a strange name for a ferret – but Kemp, Kemp was aware that Keats was wrong when he called his love-sick snake lady Lamia. A lamia was a hell-bent, blood-drinking soul, a demon spirit that came to the house at nightfall and supped upon the souls of those who dwelled there. A lamia was a vampire, but one who drained the very body essence, the very soul of its prey. Kemp was correct in naming such a beast Lamia. It was a good name. It was a correct name.

She touched the bars and peered out at Kemp as he strode down the orchard towards her. Her kind had long served folk like Kemp. She came from an ancient family – a family that had spawned bears and dogs as well as her fellow stoats. Bears and dogs had sprung from the same stock, but one line of the tree had gone awry perhaps, one line had borne the mustelids – the stoats, the weasels, the otters, the forever-angry wolverine. Two or maybe three thousand years ago, men had captured Lamia's ancestors, had drawn them, furious and foetid, from their lairs and tamed them. It had not been an easy task, the taking of those first wild polecats. They had spat and bitten and the air had become full of a pungent, clinging vapour, for the ancients had called the polecat the foulmarten, and for good reason. They had tamed readily, however, and their offspring had been quiet, gentle and easily handled. But polecats are beasts with two-fold souls. Those first tame polecats, not tame enough to call ferrets, had quickly gentled and allowed their human owners to handle them. Yet two essences of their wild forefathers had remained: the putrid smell they emitted when ruffled or hurt, and a furious psychotic disposition when they encountered small mammals or birds. These they would slay until they were exhausted, ripping and tearing into their bodies, slaying for the pure joy of killing, butchering long after hunger was surfeited. Why men first decided to tame them was a mystery, but then, Lamia had much in common with men and their ways.

Kemp approached this darting, quicksilver beast and tossed a chicken head in to the creature. He tarried a while, watching the fierce gluttony, the almost gloating possessiveness with which Lamia attacked the head, her sharp teeth gritting into the bones of the skull. Kemp trilled his fingers across the bars and seemed pleased to see that she hissed protectively over her bloody meal. 'Work for you tomorrow, my love. Work, though I would bet you'll find it a bit of a curious game. One to your liking, though,' he chuckled, the laugh strangely foreign to him.

That night he set to and fed Vogel a quarter-crop of raw hare, meat from a hare he had shot last season and frozen. A quarter-crop barely eased the fiery hunger that beset her stomach, and she craned her neck forward like a foolish stork to watch the hand that had fed her the meat. Kemp watched her, and his face lit to a watery smile. He stroked her beak with a hen's feather and watched her fiery, Argus eye. 'Peace, my sweeting, peace. Tomorrow, if you fly well and true, you'll dine on meat that's fresher by far than the food I've fed you. Peace, my sweeting.' But there was no peace in the awful, furious bird that sat upon his fist.

In the drain, Lepus began to experience the first horrors of claustrophobia. At first he lay in the cool dampness, panting, oblivious to everything save the fact that he was free from the aerial bombardment he had suffered. For an hour he lay there, breathing deeply, licking the gore that seeped from a score or more punctures, cleaning his torn ear with his fore-paws, rubbing his sore and punctured head against the side of the drain. An hour he lay there, recuperating, and then the whole horror of being enclosed burst upon him. Five or so million years had passed since the common stock that had borne both hares and rabbits had fled to earths and subterranean lairs in times of trouble. Now he was ill at ease in his confinement. Restlessly he checked each end of the drain, desperately trying to scratch away the stone, to nudge it with his head in order to move it, but Kemp had blocked the drain with his usual care and there was no escape. First light found Lepus gazing out through a crack in the barrier, fitfully scratching at the fissure.

Kemp went to his mews early the next morning. He gazed at Vogel a few moments, exultant in the fact that the famished bird bated towards him. 'Ready, are we?' he asked rhetorically. He took his ferret box and walked to the bottom of the orchard to where Lamia paced within her cage. He stroked her for a while as if the stroking reassured both man and ferret of the other's intentions, and then he boxed her ready to carry. Kemp returned to the mews where Vogel bated to his fist. 'All hell's afoot now,' he muttered to himself with satisfaction.

Lepus listened to the footfalls and the jangling sound of bells for five minutes before Kemp arrived. He edged back into the centre of the drain as if the darkness within was the key to safety. The floor of the earth stank. A badger, wounded in a road accident, had kennelled there for one night, leaking blood and filth into the drain sediment, giving the centre of the drain a rank, musty, danger-filled smell. Lepus sat, ears almost erect and touching the roof of the drain, awaiting danger.

As light showed at the end of the drain nearest the wood's perimeter, Lamia began to sniff at the edges of the hole with careful, unhurried enthusiasm, like a gourmet savouring a rare claret. She trundled into the drain towards Lepus, sniffing in the delicious odours of fear and blood. She had not scented hare before, save for a road-casualty beast which Kemp had once thrown her, but the scent of fear – a scent common to all species – was no stranger to her. She thrived on such scent, the very odour giving strength to her savage soul. Lamia trundled up the drain towards the bewildered hare. There was seemingly little to fear from this diminutive, ponderous little beast, but race memories stirred within Lepus, warning him that the dark shape meant him harm. He edged away from it towards the other end of the drain and began to scratch furiously at the stones.

'She's on him now, Vogel, watch now! Watch!' And Kemp directed Vogel's gaze towards the enclosed end of the drain.

Lamia's slow gait had increased, and in seconds she had found Lepus. Frantically she crawled over his back to deliver the cervical bite – a bite that would cripple or kill the terrified hare. Twice she climbed his rump, only to be kicked off again by a tremendous hind kick – a kick that shot her back down the drain a clear yard or more, but stoats and stoat kin are relentless foes, and she attacked the mountainous flanks with increased fervour. Kemp heard the screams and loosened the stones with his foot, levering them back to give Lepus a chance to run. The hare stood a moment, head out of the drain, as if deciding whether the fear of man, and his bell-jangling bird, was greater than that of the creeping, biting beast which sought to climb up his back. With a gargantuan effort he bounded from the earth, the ferret riding his back like a leech. In two strides he was heading for the wood edge, and rolling suddenly to dislodge the ferret. At that moment Kemp cast Vogel.

Once again Lepus heard those tinkling bells, and he redoubled his speed. Vogel flew fast and true, her belly crying out for the meat that raced ahead of her. She climbed a rise and disappeared from Kemp's sight, and the man, running rapidly to watch the flight, came upon the hawk furiously footing a screaming, shrieking prey – a prey that released a vile and pungent odour into the cold morning air. Kemp watched impotently as the hawk crushed out the life from the screeching ferret. There was little he could do. In the wood, Lepus had ceased to run and was cleaning his wounds once more and chinning.

'There'll be other times, my pretty,' said Kemp testily, lifting the mangled and dead ferret. 'There'll be other times, be sure of that.'

Lepus continued to browse.

They came suddenly that autumn, their ill-kept vans drawing heavily decorated caravans which spewed forth filth and children upon the common at Cotters End. Brennan groaned aloud, and with reason. During the waning days of September his crippled bitch had come in season, and Brennan had found her a mate in Melkham, a dog greyhound that had run at the local flapping track, an indifferent runner but a fast dog and a stayer when he had a mind to be. Now his bitch's belly began to swell with pups, a target that would attract the tinker youths like a magnet.

'Damn them! Damn them all to hell,' Brennan had muttered. 'If I had my way, tonight you'd be able to read a newspaper by the light of blazing tinker caravans.'

'Some of your people on the common,' he had taunted Harvey spitefully. 'Brings a hint of nostalgia, all that shit and axle grease, doesn't it?'

'Ain't ours,' sniffed Harvey, realizing Brennan was trying to rile him. 'Pikies, those. Speaks different, acts different.'

'Yes,' said Brennan, almost sagely. 'They rob you in Shelta, whereas your lot steal in Romany.'

'They're diddies, nothing to do with us. Hedge wumpers, good for nothing, no good to man nor beast.'

'Consoling that, Harvey, very consoling, considering that I have to leave my cottage all day to the tender mercies of that bunch of bastards.'

'When you can see 'em they do you no harm, Brennan. It's when they go and come back you'll find trouble. If they are to screw your place, they'll do it a week or so after they leave.'

Thus the unwelcome, unwanted band came to settle at Cotters End – a loathsome, dirty, illiterate, thieving band, though they had not always been so. Four hundred years before this band had still boasted descent from Culain the Smith, for during the great days of Saint David and Saint Patrick the band had drifted around Ireland, famous for their nomadic ways and their skill in working iron. Four hundred years since they might still have boasted that they had forged the spear-head of the legendary Gae Bolg, the terrible belly spear of Cuchulain, but now such talk had slithered into a mire of forgetfulness and indifference as to their origins. The band might have stayed in Ireland, mending pots and selling ponies who had a reputation for being able to jump the moon, but there came a time when the potato haulms withered under the blight, the tubers rotted in the barn, and common folk found difficulty in staying alive, let alone condoning the ways of the nomads. Thus the band had drifted into England, speaking Shelta, a bastard Irish tongue, full of borrowed words, the jargon of the outcast and the oppressed.

The band had bred freely with outsiders, though only those who were more lawless and more delinquent than the tinkers sought to marry into such a group. Outcast Romanies, those outlawed for perversion and murder, joined them and mated with them – imparting a dark hue to the band; but most of the new blood came from shiftless, restless folk given to thieving and violence rather than work. The grandfather of the band at Cotters End had been a 'moucher' from Cambridge, a man given to scrounging, poaching and petty theft, a man who had jumped the budget and set up home with a half-bred Romany tinker woman. Borrow had seen this band early in the 1800s and had been alarmed at their villainy. They had declined still further since.

Within moments of their arrival on the common, the landscape had become a rubbish heap of tyres, car carcasses and scrap iron, and the youths had begun to plague the neighbourhood. As Brennan had predicted, it would only be a matter of time before an offer was made for his pregnant, crippled bitch. 'Would you be after selling the little dog, sir?' (Strange, thought Brennan, how they manage to make the term 'sir' sound offensive, and he wondered whether 'sir' wasn't the tinker equivalent of the Romany 'Gorgio' – a derogatory word, meaning 'outsider'.)

'Best to give 'em what they ask. They'll only come back for things and do damage as well as steal,' Harvey had said, but Brennan was unlikely to trade his damaged bitch anyway.

'Give you a puppy come spring,' he lied, hoping they would go away.

'Keep you to it, sir, keep you to it,' said the youths, and returned to the filthy quagmire that only a few days before had been Cotters End Common.

The common now boasted a host of dogs: terriers, curs and lurchers all showing signs of oil stains and neglect. Mange was always present in the bobbery band, and children and dogs alike scratched incessantly. Lice, fleas and scabies would always be fellow travellers of the band, as much an insignia of the people as were the untaxed, uninsured vans. One dog alone stood out as being less oil-stained, less verminous than the others, a tall, heavily built, brindle greyhound, earmarked with an Irish marker, though the Ireland that had bred him was a different world from the Ireland that had spawned the travellers. Dogs of kings, the forest laws had called the greyhound, and now the dog of kings stuck out incongruously in the filth of the tinker settlement. He didn't belong there, neither did he wish to belong there.

He had been whelped in Kerry out of an open race bitch that hadn't quite made it to the top league but had been well enough bred and trier enough to be a good prospect to perpetuate her illustrious blood-line. She had run her days on the licensed tracks, and when her speed had begun to wane, she had been retired 'to brood'. A half-dozen dogs had served her, and her progeny, while not exceptional, had been good, and the brindle dog from her last mating had been considered a fair prospect. He had been allowed complete liberty during the golden days of his youth, allowed to run the farm, to quarter in the hay-ricks. There had been food in plenty always available, for whelps that are to run well must feed well. Thus, as a sapling, he had been auctioned as 'Bellweather' and sold to a racer in Nantwich, Cheshire, for two hundred guineas – a fair price for an untried whelp, but, considering his lineage, not a large price.

Parry had bought him out of a bonus he had made while working on the motorway, though it had not been a chance purchase, for Parry was no stranger to the world of greyhound racing. Bellweather had been groomed and tended well, fed the best regardless of expense, and raced lightly until his measure was known. It took Parry little time to realize the potential of the dog, to realize that, properly tended, he had speed enough to whip all on the flapping tracks of that area. Thus Bellweather, raced occasionally as Parry's Lad, had topped all contenders in the field for miles around. Parry had boasted of the dog's ability often – once too often, it transpired.

He had walked his dog, muzzled and on a short leash, down the High Street of his village one Saturday. The beast had been a picture of health, a strong, powerful four-year-old, still with another year or so of his best in him. Parry was proud of him and justly so; for the last three years, he had been Parry's thoughts in waking and sleeping.

A grubby Bedford pick-up had pulled up alongside him and, in a familiar Irish lilt, a voice had inquired, 'Is he for sale, mister?' Parry had shaken his head. 'Will he tak a hare, mister, tak a hare?'

Parry had laughed at the question, amazed as to how these clowns could question that the fastest dog in Cheshire could be beaten by a hare. 'Of course,' he had replied, and walked home, forgetting the incident.

Parry knew much of greyhounds, but little of the ways of tinkers, it transpired. That night Bellweather had been taken, the locks of the shed broken and the dog led away to the pick-up. It was a pity really. The dog had seen hares, but only the clockwork, predictable variety that run a circular predictable route, always at a regulated speed. He had never seen the kind that could bob, weave, jink, adjust its speed in a trice and break the heart of any running dog. It was of the latter variety he was about to learn.

Autumn had trickled into a foul, muddy winter – wet rather than cold, and the berries of the hawthorn bushes growing soft and rotten before the spring would come.

'Curious things – berries,' Harvey had said. 'If they fall on the ground and rot away, it's a year or more before they shoot and send up greens. If a bird eats them, the seed'll pass through in the shit and they'll be up and growing within a month.'

Brennan had glanced up without answering, his mind filled with tinkers rather than hawberries. It had been a year of mud, a wet summer followed by a wet and mild winter, a time of rotting, a time of disease, Harvey had said, for few well-fed beasts sicken during the cold of a hard winter, but a wet winter sees all manner of troubles abroad.

Across the bridge in the meadows near Brookhay, Lepus was feeding on a patch of sowthistle, grown rank and luscious in the damp, mild winter. He chinned the prickly prongs and stretched. All marks of the conflict with Vogel had long since disappeared and only tiny ticks of white remained to show where her talons had punctured his hide, seeking out the viscera. One ear remained a little askew, for during the tumbling battle with the goshawk her hind claw, a hooked scimitar of a claw, had punctured the ear muscles that held the pinna upright, and now Lepus would go through life with one ear held at a slightly ridiculous angle. The winter had been kind to him, for the herbage continued to grow long after the time when frosts should have made a living hard to get. He was troubled somewhat with coccidia, an organism that sometimes infected his liver during the mild winters, but hares had always been plagued with coccidia, it was no new thing.

Life was easy for him. The estate on which he fed was lightly 'shot over' and keepered to prevent poachers running it. Twice only that autumn had he been run, both times with small, nondescript lurchers lacking class and speed, their efforts irritating rather than frightening him. He had been casual with them, assessing their potential, and finally outpacing them as if contemptuous of their efforts. His cocked ear and his black stripe made him conspicuous, however, and he was rapidly becoming a legend on the other side of the bridge, and for a hare to become such a legend is to court tragedy.

One night at the Plough, Vickery had spoken of him. 'D'you know there's a little black-striped jack on the estate? The little sod'll take some bloody catching. Me cousin's lads come up last Monday and ran him nigh to hell with the lurcher dogs. Ran him. Should have seen him go. No bigger'n a rabbit, but he thrashed them dogs up hill and down dale. Be surprised if there's a dog in Britain to take the little sod.'

Tapper, the barman, had shied away from Vickery's bad breath, uttering, 'Aye, it's a good dog that'll take a hare round here. A green 'un, a young 'un, well, that's one thing, but one that knows dogs and fields, one who's at home on land will take some catching, what with hedges, dry walls and such like.'

Tapper considered himself an expert on hares and their ways; he had been hearing hunters talk nonsense about them for years now.

Two of the tinker youths listened and finished their beer. 'Is it a hare you're saying that can't be caught,' – and added as a sort of sting – 'Sir?' Tapper ignored them. When the tinkers came in number he refused to serve them, for their presence didn't actually encourage the summer visitors and the boating people on whom his business largely depended. 'Is it a hare you're saying that can't be caught?' the youth repeated.

Vickery, who felt strangely at home with anyone even dirtier than himself, replied, 'Yes, a little black-striped jack that lives on the Colonel's estate.' And added cautiously, 'You'd need permission to run him, though, the estate is keepered.'

The youth smiled at the absurdity of the statement. His group lived outside the law, failing to pay taxes, to insure vehicles, and going wherever they pleased. If they were arrested they gave their names as James Brown, a panacea against arrest, suffered a few blows from the police and vanished before prosecution could start. Even Vickery began to smile, a black-toothed grin, at the stupidity of the statement.

'Is it on the Colonel's estate you say, sir?' the youth repeated, seemingly aware of Vickery's delight at being addressed as anything other than Vickery.

Tapper shook his head. 'Watch it! the bastards will be swarming over the estate tomorrow, the sodding nuisances.'

As the sun rose the youths had tied the great brindled hound on a slip of binder twine and, together with half a dozen other curs, they strode towards the meadows of the estate. The dog was in ragged condition, for, contrary to country legends, few tinkers keep their animals in style, doctoring them with herbal nostrums to get the best out of them. Bellweather had lived a careful rationed life with Parry, feeding on boiled beef and brown bread soaked in the meat juice. Among the tinkers his fare was less generous. He ate while there was

- THE TINKERS' BRINDLE -

food, gorging until bursting, and fasting when there was none, and the fast periods had become all too common. The downy gloss had long left his coat, and his irregular, unbalanced diet had made his gut inflamed. Two ribs showed as they had when he won his first major race, but such condition had once been brought about by judicious deprivation prior to the race – now it was a condition wrought by neglect.

'Hound'll take him easy, faster than a lurcher,' murmured one of the youths knowingly. They opened the gate and the curs rioted into the field, chasing rabbits to cover, flushing partridges, at which the tinkers threw a cascade of stones. A moment or so later the curs had quietened, and were casting about in the long grass for scent – scent that was muffled since their coats held the smell of diesel oil. A yearling leveret near Barratt's Covert lay low in the grass, hoping to escape detection, crouching lower as the band approached, head sitting into its neck, ears to its back. The curs feathered the ground near it, questing frantically now.

'On one now. Get ready to slip der hound.'

At last the leveret could stand the tension no longer and leaped into flight. The hound had never seen a live hare, but that which moved was for chasing, and for that he had been bred. He lurched forward, clear of his slip. In spite of his poor condition, his speed was great, and he closed with the fleeing leveret, experiencing the same wild exhilaration he had felt when he had closed with the bobbing track hare. He reached down to snap up the furry shape, but at the moment of impact the leveret jinked and the hound overshot by ten yards. He turned rapidly, gaining on the dancing leveret once more; again he reached, again he missed, again he overshot.

'Should've had 'im then,' sniffed the oldest youth bitterly. 'The bugger's no good.'

Three times the giant hound turned the leveret off the hedge, a dozen times he missed the strike. He was near to being winded when Lepus got up, startled by the course in the field.

Lepus had short law, a dozen yards or a little more, when the hound saw him, changing quarry from the leveret to Lepus. A dozen yards was a short enough distance for an indifferent lurcher to take a hare, but Bellweather was winded now with a great fiery ache in his lung cavity – an ache that increased by the stride. He closed with Lepus, snapping at the tiny shape that danced before him, nimble as a fencing master. Twice he bowled him, twice he reached for him, only to snap at thin air as Lepus rolled effortlessly to avoid the collision. Bellweather was weary now and every muscle ached, but he had been trained to go on. Two hundred years previously, Lord Orford had crossed Bellweather's ancestors with fierce, gutsy fighting bulldogs, the sort that feared nothing. The sting, the do-or-die attitude, still prevailed in the running dogs. He had been bred to run, bred to give his best, bred to continue even though his muscles ached and his chest was on fire. At Hartman's stile he turned Lepus back into the field again, losing twelve yards in the turn, unaware of the ways of hares, unaware of the manner of their running. Twice he gained on the hare as they raced through the dingles in the centre of the field, dingles caused by the subsidence of the limestone caves far below the surface. Twice he reached, twice he missed by a yard.

He had been hard put when Lepus got up. Now he was exhausted, but he had been bred to go on, bred from the gutsiest to the gutsiest. No quitter appeared in his family tree. His pedigree was written in raw courage. He stayed with his adversary, every stride an agony. At Langham Hollow he struck a single strand of barbed wire, but such was his weight, such was his speed, that it burst asunder with a twang, scarcely slowing the brindle dog a second. His eyes were dim now and the tiny shape darted in front of him in a red mist, always one step ahead, always an inch outside the reach of that chopping mouth. Fresh, unwinded, he might have taken Lepus, snatched at him in that first burst, smashed his tiny rib cage in that rat-trap jaw, but he was not fresh. Now he was fading rapidly. He turned Lepus once more, and they raced back towards the dingles, the hound's breath coming as a hot, rasping gasp. He saw the hollows, gained ground and reached for the hare, but a great blackness overwhelmed him and he crashed earthwards; yet he had been bred to chase, bred to endure hardship, bred to take the knocks and injuries a chase offered. He rose, swaying like an aspen in the breeze, and continued. There was no hare now, just a bobbing blur that continued to outpace him. He fell again, and his heaving sides continued to quiver, the hind legs paddling as if to prevent drowning. He thrashed a while and lay still.

The tinkers converged on the greyhound. 'No good! The lying bastard said he was a bloody good hare dog. Lying bastard!' The youth kicked the carcass savagely. 'Sodding hare dog. Ha, the black-striped bugger's killed 'im.'

But with the death of the great hound Lepus became a legend.

Thus, with the demise of the great brindled greyhound, the legend of Lepus began. Stories of him grew with time, silly stories about supernatural speed and cunning became common, but with fame of this kind came further danger. Bands of louts, lurchers on slips, invaded his territory almost daily, and the Colonel, for all his prosecutions of poachers, was unable to prevent the harassment of hares on his estate. Every hunter who owned a running dog worthy of being called a lurcher began to hunt the land, each one eager to be known as the one who had slain the black-striped hare. Throughout the summers they ran his does, heavy with young, their pregnancy making them easy for the taking; they butchered his leverets, too young to outpace the dogs, and ran him incessantly. How he survived was a miracle, but each spring would find him duelling with other jacks in the water meadows, furious at his rivals, and each year found a fresh crop of leverets, each with a dark spinal patch.

Harvey watched impersonally as the seasons passed, observing Brennan becoming more bitter by the day at his lot in life, in conflict with himself as much as with society, watching and regretting the houses that encroached upon the fields at Cotters End. And Harvey, in watching, wore his own homespun philosophy, a philosophy so deep and complex that Brennan, for all his reading, could not fathom it. All forces worked in harmony in Harvey's world, whereas Brennan found it necessary to hate and make war on his fellow man and on a society that restricted him.

One evening, while he was sharpening some cutting tools for Tapper, Harvey spoke to Brennan about the hare. 'You know, Brennan, fame of his kind is a heller. All out to get him. Ain't it best to pass through life inconspicuous, rolling with the breeze, so to speak.'

'Uneasy lies the head that wears the crown, you mean,' quipped Brennan. 'Shit, Harvey, you're a right little ecologist. Crediting a hare with human sentiments now, is it? Each time he's run it's another tussle to him – he doesn't see it as a vendetta against him. Beasts don't think like that. Perhaps beasts don't think for that matter. Anyway, where the hell have you got the idea that society is conducting a war against a hare? Who in God's name conducts a vendetta against a wild beast?'

'You, for one, I think. Reckon it's the only reason you bred Czar.'

Brennan spat out an insult at the Romany, who seemed unusually content at the way the grindstone scored sparks from a sickle as it honed the edges of the blade. 'You're getting crazier as you get older, Harvey,' he uttered, and went on idly stroking the ears of his sapling lurcher.

Czar was tall for a puppy of this breeding, favouring his sire rather than his dam in size, but the coat was soft, long and linty, more like that of the old blind bitch in Harvey's yard. Brennan gazed at the dog in admiration, much as Pygmalion had gazed at the statue in the vineyards of Cyprus. Czar's head was broad and powerful, the jaws immense, but his real strength lay in the knotted muscles of his hind legs, enormous cords of tissue that would expand and harden still more.

'You get a sort of kick out of stroking that beast, almost worship the thing,' Harvey muttered.

Brennan ignored him, realizing there was some truth in the statement.

'A mite ungodly, if you ask me,' Harvey continued.

'No one is asking you, Harvey, no one is,' whispered Brennan, still fondling the silky tassels of the dog's ears.

The dog had grown into a miracle of beauty, a joy to behold, and he had taken to training like a duck to water. At four months old he had been able to hunt, head down, quartering the land like a hound, and his obedience was such that even Harvey, ever ready to sell any of Brennan's achievements short, had remarked on the dog's intelligence. Collie blood had given it 'eye' and intelligence, the sagacity to realize what Brennan wanted of it, and some unknown breed lost in the ancestry of the beast had ensured that the nose would be acute. From his numerous greyhound ancestors came speed and an agility that could match a whippet. Each morning that speed and strength increased. Each day saw an increase in his bushcraft and stamina. At seven months of age, he had been snatching up rabbits lying too far from the corn, rabbits which he retrieved live to hand when Brennan was with him, but killed and ate when he poached the Cotters End fields by himself. He was a yearling now, and already a good prospect as a coursing dog. A shade tall for some, but with his height went a stride that ate up the distance between him and the quarry.

Brennan caressed the dog's ears once more. 'Teach you the lamp next week, as soon as the moon is down. Sharpen you for the coursing and get you to understand how to pick up a running beast. I'll jump you again this weekend. Take you up to eight feet if necessary now that your pasterns are set. There won't be a hedge for miles that you won't jump by this time next week. Ten weeks from now you'll catch hares, I promise you, and then, when you get to know the sport, when you've skill enough, we'll butcher the little black-striped sod.'

Harvey listened to Brennan's diatribe, shaking his head sagely. Having known Brennan for some time he was used to his ways, his convoluted manner of thinking, his bitter, spiteful ripostes when hurt. Yet somehow this passion to kill the hare was foreign to Brennan's make-up.

'Reckon he's finally a bit round the twist,' thought Harvey secretly. 'The damned hare won't let him rest. The business needs to be finished, one way or another.'

George Beddows slapped the side of his riding boot with his silver-headed crop. 'Damn! One thing after another. Taking the Colonel's nephew as a whip might have given us all the land between Barkstone and Dreville, but he's far too keen at playing tunes on that horn to be much use to the bloody beagles. Still, it's new country to hunt and what with the housing development choking the countryside, any new country is not to be sniffed at. Have to find a way to tell that boy not to play cornet solos on his bloody horn, though. Never pick an ex-Scout as a whip, George, me boy. With your luck it's ten to one the bloke will be a bugler.'

George lolled back in his leather upholstered armchair. No, luck had never been unkind to him, not by a long chalk. Three hundred years ago one of his ancestors had come to work at Bannerton Hall as a hedger and since then there had always been Beddows at Bannerton Hall. The estate had changed hands several times, but the Beddows had been kept on for they were as much a part of the estate as the walls of Bannerton itself, and they could lay claim to a far longer family tree than the hall's present owners, and no less illustrious either. Young, the village historian, had once described the family in his most pretentious manner as 'typical of the British yeomanry, the very backbone of English rural life', a worn old cliché but one which George's father had relished. There had been a Beddows in Marlborough's army that had raced to battle at Blenheim, and a Beddows had lent respectability to the 'infamous army' who fought at Waterloo. 'Typical English yeomanry' just about described the family, each member of which seemed devoid of ambition, content to live out their days with enough rather than striving to have plenty. All George's ancestors had served at Bannerton Hall as farmworkers, coachmen, handymen; a great-uncle had even risen to the exalted rank of second footman. It was indeed curious that such a family had produced George, for George was decidedly different.

Some people are born with what is called in hackneyed terms the Midas touch, the ability to turn the most muddled and unprofitable enterprise into a thriving concern, and George was certainly one of those who possessed this strange and rare quality. School had bored him, and he had found the acquisition of useless information, the learning of pointless facts, a meaningless chore. He had been dubbed as average by his teachers, a 'could do better if he tried' type of pupil, and at fifteen he had left school to take up work at a local garage owned by a giant of a man called Miller, a man as deep in debt as he was in his cups. The garage had been a ramshackle affair of galvanised sheeting that shimmered with heat in the summer and froze its workers during the winter. George had watched this fairly thriving concern accelerate on the downhill path to bankruptcy, but the study of its decline and of Miller's uselessness had taught him much on how not to run a business.

At seventeen, by dint of thrift and a willingness to work well into the night on cars of his own, George had amassed enough capital to start up his own garage, buying up an equally ramshackle business some two miles from Bannerton Hall. Miller had been reluctant to pay bills, tardy at meeting his commitments, sloppy in his workmanship, disinclined to be punctual in anything other than attending the six o'clock opening time call. George had outworked and undercut the drunkard and his garage prospered so rapidly that by the age of twenty he employed two men nearly twice his age. He invested his capital buying and selling used cars and his manner, neither subservient nor brash, lent itself to the trade. Furthermore, his rural background and upbringing had taught him a certain honesty in dealing with people – a quality much admired and sadly seldom associated with used car dealers. His business had prospered – no, prospered seems hardly adequate. It had boomed, and soon he owned a dozen or so garages and showrooms.

His failure to make a 'go' of his marriage might have been the only 'down spot' of Beddows' success-filled life, but even in this he seemed to come out on top. He had left his wife, the daughter of a wealthy farmer and a woman of independent means, but even after the divorce she remained on speaking terms with him and she made few financial claims on him. He still visited her long after she married a local publican, but after the failure of his marriage he devoted himself entirely to work, working eighteen or more hours a day, tumbling into bed exhausted, rising at dawn to start another eventful and usually very profitable day. When his friends had ridiculed his way of life and tried to prise him away from his work with the old adage 'All work and no play', he had simply laughed and said, 'A quick million and I'm out, I promise.'

His friends had laughed at his prophecy, but by the age of thirty-three he had made his quick but hard-earned million and, true to his work, had got out.

Even after his retirement, his Midas touch prevailed. In whatever businesses he invested his money, they made a huge and handsome profit. Somehow or other he just couldn't put a foot wrong. He bought Bannerton Hall, renovated its crumbling stonework, replaced the ancient, rotting woodwork that woodworm and mould had turned into dust, and when he had found the hall too cold for his needs, too big for his requirements, he sold it for double the price given. He felt almost ashamed of his prosperity, almost vulgar about the fact that all his ventures prospered. 'You got more money than George Beddows,' became a local saying, a saying that embarrassed him a little, though he had to admit it also gave him a certain sense of pride, a sense of achievement perhaps.

His life was now a kaleidoscope of women. Once his marriage was dissolved, women found his personal charm as attractive as the fact that he was rich. It was difficult not to like Beddows, and even rival car dealers who had 'gone under' through his acute business sense had to admit a certain sneaking liking for the man. All admitted that, in spite of his quick tongue, George just didn't have the ability to be hurtful.

Remarriage didn't seem a very good idea to him, however, and since his energy still prevailed, uncramped by the inactivity of retirement, he became actively involved in the social life of the country. He took to field sports, becoming an accomplished falconer, succeeding well in flying imported Spanish peregrines at grouse upon the Scottish moors, but the sport of falconry offered little of the social bustle that had been part and parcel of his hectic business life, and after mastering the sport he found it palling on him somewhat. It was a sport requiring patience and skill of a sort, but it was the sport of the solitary, the loner, and George was intensely gregarious. He needed an active social life more than a sporting life.

Thus he was drawn into what he chose to call the 'county set', the world of the hunts and all the social accoutrement that accompanied the world of fox hunting. For a while, the fox-hunting fraternity found his abrasive dynamism, his brash, though likeable, extrovert disposition a little disconcerting. He made no pretence of having what is called in such circles 'breeding' – he had none, and pretence was hardly his forte. To compensate for his lack of that most intangible quality, though, he had a very obvious charisma, and what was more, he had wealth. After a while folk forgot his *nouveau riche* attitude and accepted him. However, he could not ride, having a childhood fear of horses, and this in itself proved an obstacle. To a man of George's abilities, however, it was not insurmountable. He took lessons from the best of teachers, employed a stud groom who had seen service with the Quorn and who, in addition to keeping Beddows's horses in the pink, taught him the social niceties associated with hunting. From his groom he learned to differentiate between 'gentlemen farmers' and merely gentlemen who were invited to wear pink at various hunts. He learned how not to make a *faux pas* by addressing a scarlet-coated Master as 'Huntsman', and with perseverance began to scale the snooty social ladder of the hunting fraternity, a social hierarchy which money alone could not buy.

It was, at first, a steep climb. His parents were regarded as somewhat rustic by the local land-owners, and his absence of good schooling was patently obvious when he spoke. It took him a little time to realize that, in spite of the airs and graces of many of the hunt, wits-wise he was able to buy and sell them. Thus, after the initial ice had been broken, he progressed from strength to strength. His gift of acquiring any woman he wished made him 'a bit of a feller', and his ability to hold his liquor made him a person to envy. Altogether, Beddows seemed to have been cut out for the obligatory social life associated with the hunt.

For a matter of two years he rode to hounds three and sometimes four times a week, and his superbly tailored clothes and immaculately turned-out horses soon won over the most stand-offish of the hunting fraternity. He climbed that social ladder in leaps rather than in the hand-over-hand laborious manner which most of the newly wealthy used. Within three years he had been elected Master, or rather joint Master, the then Master being an old and crusty judge known for his ability to settle both horses and juries. Again George's enormous vitality carried him everywhere. He became an accoutrement – what the well-dressed dinner party should invite – and if his days were spent hunting, his nights were spent in an incessant roundelay of dinner parties. His constitution, that he rated as hard as iron, began to suffer from this terrific pounding, and he developed gastric troubles and experienced violent headaches, even on the days when he did not hunt. At first he attributed his blinding headaches and nausea to the fact that he jumped his horses at near-impossible obstacles, crashing through hedges the like of which other members of the field avoided or simply waited by until Beddows cleared the way. The compulsory social life of the hunt bit into his pocket a little but attacked his constitution even harder.

One morning he had heaved himself up onto his horse with a little more effort than he usually required. It puzzled him. Admittedly, the last few days had been an incredible social whirl, and he had slept little or not at all. But then he usually lived this way. He could remember his huntsmen trotting slowly towards him in an action-replay, slow-motion trot, and could distinctly recall the fact that the hounds seemed unusually brightly coloured. After this he remembered nothing, not even the crashing earthwards from his panic-stricken mount, the hurried ambulance race to the local hospital, the month in the intensive care and coronary unit. He had imbibed the sweet smell of success quite easily, but he found the bitter taste of mortality a little more difficult to stomach.

His doctor was appalled when George described the way he lived, the amount he drank, the hectic whirl of his social life, and he left Beddows in no doubt whatsoever that the liquor and constant parties had to cease. He prescribed an alcohol-free diet, regular meals and even more regular exercise. To caution an ebullient, effervescent original such as George about his social life was like trying to tame a March wind, and after the initial horror of the coronary had worn off, Beddows crept back to his social life once more. Nay, he increased it. He needed exercise, the doctor had said. Thus he bought himself a private pack of beagles, and two days a week he ran with his hounds, far exceeding the gentle exercise prescribed by his doctor.

Beagling is unique among the hound-hunting field sports, for it puts as great a strain on the huntsman as on the hounds. Some days he would hunt his diminutive hounds for five hours, returning as exhausted as they were, sometimes falling asleep in the beagle kennels to be put to bed by his groom. His constitution tottered for a while, and then regained equilibrium, the coronary becoming a thing to be joked about rather than never mentioned. He became the social hunter pure and simple, most interested in the social life, the pageantry, the almost archaic rituals associated with hunting. He was the least predatory of men, regretting each and every hare slain, saddened rather than exhilarated by the kill. Thus his small private pack of beagles might have become a fun pack, and the 'meet' an event as anti-climactic as a drag hunt, a pack that didn't really worry if it killed or not. It might have been had he not purchased Bantam. Bantam changed all that, for if George lacked the hunting instinct, Bantam had more than enough for the two. He was that sort of hound. Very soon Beddows realized that he no longer hunted the pack. He was simply a whip to Bantam.

- BANTAM -

Bantam lay upon his bench and yawned. Once, during the early days of the pack, his dark tri-colour colouring and small size made him conspicuous, but now nearly all the pack was his colour. Nearly all the pack was of his getting. Pedlar, a yearling hound, approached him, fawning, turning his head in an appeasement gesture, mindful of the patriarch's position. Bantam half lifted his lips and snarled. He had grown crotchety in his later years, and such was his skill in the field that Beddows never punished him when he struck at a puppy. He was old now, old for a beagle required to run for five hours through plough and pasture, over hedge and hillock, and his muzzle was greying. Yet he was the pride of the pack. 'The Treasure', George called him, promising him that he would sleep out his last years next to the fire in Beddows' hall. He was not always rated so highly, however.

His breeding was 'of the purple'. His sire, Chorister, was a pale tan and white stallion hound, a looker who had won well at Peterborough, but whose strength lay in the field and in his quality of being able to stamp nose and stamina into his progeny. He had run six years with the Courtney, and his hunting quality was of the best – so good, in fact, that few packs in the three counties had not used him to cover their bitches, and a rash of pale tan and white hounds predominated in the local packs. Bantam's dam was Vanity, as good a bitch as the Courtney had ever bred. She would live to run eight seasons with the pack, never causing riot, always in at the kill, and seemingly tireless at the end of the longest hunt. Her nose was unerring. Often, when scent was poor and the pack feathered aimlessly and foolishly, Courtney would say, 'Let's see what Vanity says,' and he would treat the opinion of the old matron with respect, and rightly so. Vanity was never known to lie.

But nose was not the only quality that Bantam inherited from his parents. A hundred years before this strain had been crossed with fiery, bull terrier-blooded dogs, the beagle blood being used to impart voice and sense to the progeny, to produce fox-hunting terriers who would stay to annoy and tease a fox from its earth or to pin a fierce, old boar badger in its lair, denning it, fixing it, so the diggers could delve to the beast. There was no shortage of courage in the line, that was for certain. Above all, the Courtney line was famed for its stamina, a grinding, relentless stamina that knew no bottom, a stamina that would carry the hounds through the shadowy world of fatigue and exhaustion to a kill, a stamina well suited to the grinding, ruthless war of attrition that men call beagling. In truth, Bantam had been bred in the purple. It was curious he had grown as he did.

His dam had whelped him in the May, a good time to bear whelps, a warm time, a time for growing, those first days of summer. Five whelps she had borne, and Bantam was the smallest, a tiny tri-coloured hound who had paddled his way among his siblings to suckle the bitch. He had been born small, but smallness is not always equated with weakness. Wilde, Villa, Perez had been born tiny slivers of men with scarcely enough muscle to be considered anything more than boys, but each and every one of them had been strong enough and fit enough to weather gruelling, seemingly endless fights, battles that would have exhausted men twice or three times their weight. It is folly to equate that which is small with that which is weak, yet smallness of size is always regarded as weakness in horses and hounds. Bantam had been born small, which illustrates the error of such an assumption.

Courtney viewed the litter with a critical eye the day of the birth, watching the dam lick the squealing, suckling horde. Had Vanity borne a large litter, as she had done in her youth, he would have drowned the tiny tri-coloured hound that somehow resembled neither the dam nor the illustrious, prepotent sire. As it was, the matron had milk in plenty and was fat, so Bantam was allowed to live and grow in those warm days of summer.

He had never looked right, had never been the part as far as Courtney was concerned, and the Master came each day to view the whelp crossly, to feel increasingly dissatisfied as he grew. Had the pack been a pack of pocket beagles, the sort that entertained Mary Queen of Scots during her incarceration, he might have done, but the type of dog required to run rabbits a few scuttling yards from their earths – rabbits stunk out with burned oil and sulphur – was not the sort that men required to run hares across plough, to cascade over drystone walls, to bulldoze their way through thickets and bogs.

Each day Courtney and his kennelman Kent would view the growing litter critically. 'He won't do, Kent. He just won't do. He's too small by a damn sight. Bred properly or not, he'll make the pack look like a comic outing. He's no size or class. Look at his type. All wrong.' He shook his head sadly. 'He's all back and short legs.'

Yet when the time came when the hounds were put out to walk, Bantam was still there with the rest of the litter. It is essential that beagles should be walked – that is, put out to family homes, where they can grow up in intimate contact with people, seeing the hustle and bustle of everyday life. Hounds denied walk, reared in kennels, as are many hounds in districts where it is difficult to put them out to walk, grow well physically but are often dull and lack-lustre. Walked hounds are, by contrast, quick to learn, easy to discipline and, when they are resettled, to educate to the ways of hunting. They take to the sport with greater glee, more *joie de vivre* than hounds that are kennel reared. Thus Bantam somehow found himself at walk, though Courtney was more inclined to put him down than to put him out at walk.

The Proberts had taken the whelp – the Proberts, a rich, towny-type family that bred show Hereford cattle and daughters. It was a house overrun and dominated by women. The head of the house, head in name only, had begun life as an apprentice in a textile firm and was the epitome of the self-made man. He had married late in life to a woman twenty years his junior, and his plump and comely wife, fecund as a sow, had borne him seven daughters in the same number of years. At the age of fifty-seven, Probert had bought Laurel Green, partly to get away from the town and partly in the hope that the huge house and grounds would lose his daughters in its immensity. It was a standard joke among his fellow industrialists that Probert hated his wife and had sired so many children to lose her in the crowd. Into this world of feminine bustle and petticoat confusion came Bantam.

Against Courtney's better judgement, the hound had been put to walk with the Proberts, although neither he nor Probert had much say in the matter. One day it had rained daughters at his kennels, and Courtney had found the seven Probert children gleefully playing with the puppies. Children are hardly the best judges of dog flesh, the best connoisseurs of hounds, for they invariably single out the smallest or most weakly of the litter for their attentions. By the end of the day, Bantam was on his way to becoming a spoilt family pet and was finally saved from that fate only by his breeding. Courtney was reluctant to allow the hound to be put to walk with the family, preferring that they should take a heavily marked tan bitch of superior quality, but the children would have none of it. Finally, Courtney accepted their judgement. After all, it was wise to keep in with Probert, for not only did the stocky, soft-spoken, henpecked little man own considerable acreage, but the family had given old Barrister a home in his dotage, and old Barrister – as sweet a hound as Courtney had ever owned – was a grand old boy, too good to be put down and a special favourite with Courtney. Thus, with a shrug and a wince, Courtney allowed Bantam to be put to walk at Laurel Green. Besides, he comforted himself, they'll make such a pet of the ugly little devil that they'll be loath to return him. But Bantam was not bred to be a pet, and sooner or later blood would out.

Thus Bantam had grown up in the hurly-burly of the daughter-filled house of the Proberts, and he had submitted to and enjoyed the caresses, the games and even the dressing-up in dolls' clothes. He had grown well during the summer and autumn, but that which is not designed to be full size can rarely be persuaded into growing to full size. Bantam he had been named, a diminutive type of fowl, a name well suited to the tiny hound, but a Bantam is not merely dis-tinguished by its lack of size, its very name is equated with persistence and pluck, and if this is so, Bantam was well named. He was low to the ground and over-long in his coupling, and, as Courtney had once said, he looked more like the hounds described by Turberville than the hounds of Beckford. Periodically Courtney would visit the Probert house, though the noise and femininity of the household made the visits of this quiet, sedate bachelor a chore more than a pleasure. He could never but wince when he saw the diminutive hound greet him at the gate. He would pat the whelp, make a mental note not to repeat the mating again, and enter the awful, pink-taffeta confusion of the Probert household.

Bantam was not the only dog that shared the girls' affections since Barrister, the gaunt and scarred veteran hound, also lived out his days in the hearth of Laurel Green. Barrister had once been rated the best hound in the three counties, but, though he served numerous bitches and his progeny was scattered throughout the packs of the country, he had bred nothing of worth, nothing with his good qualities. It was as if the Almighty had allowed the blood line to build to a genetic crescendo in the old hound, and then had decided that Courtney should bring the family tree to an end. Kent had seen the mediocrity of Barrister's whelps and had comforted Courtney by saying, 'Well, sir, one thing about it, if he were to sire stock of his quality there'd be no hares left between here and the fens.'

It was perhaps true. Few packs could boast hounds of Barrister's ilk; it was Barrister who had been responsible for that famous day in 1968, a day when, though the scent was indifferent, the pack had killed three couple. It was Barrister who led the way during the famous four-hour hunt in 1971 – a hunt when the stragglers among the hounds seemed more numerous than ever – a hunt that exhausted the pack and the field, but Barrister had stayed on the hare, running it to a state of exhaustion, losing it and finding it a hundred times. It was Barrister who had out-stripped the pack and been in at the kill, alone except for a youngster who rejoined the hunt after being lost in

Netherby Woods for two hours. All in all, during his golden years, Barrister was regarded as a treasure, and if he was a poor stallion hound, he was the best of tutors.

He accepted the fawning of the whelp stoically, hating the licking and sycophantic play that is characteristic of all young hounds. When he wearied of the annoyance, when he tired of the ridiculous games, he growled, baring his gums to display his yellow, blunt eye-teeth and his shattered incisors. He had been the veteran of the kennels, sovereign of the dog hounds, and his menace was treated with respect. There had been little fighting, relatively no striving to attain social hierarchy in the kennels. A thousand years of breeding in packs, of community life, of social equilibrium had weeded out the aggressive terrier-type dogs, and harmony existed among the beagles. It needed very little for Bantam to accept the dominance of the ancient hound, and after his first week at the walk he treated the elderly dog with respect.

Both hounds were allowed total liberty, for walk without freedom is a travesty. True, Bantam was checked and cautioned when he rioted among the ornamental fowl or worried the gardener's game-cocks. Likewise he was severely thrashed for chasing the cade lamb reared by the oldest daughter – a nuisance of a beast unable to come to terms with the fact that it was a sheep and not a dog – but otherwise Bantam enjoyed total freedom. At six months of age he found pleasure in accompanying the ancient, crotchety Barrister on hunts. Barrister was old, but though senility had taken the edge off his speed and stamina, his sense of sight, hearing and above all smell had not left him. He would hunt like a basset, ponderous, with deep voice, but as exact and true as he had been during his glorious second season, a season that had convinced all of Courtney's field of the value of the hound.

It was by imitation of the ancient hound that Bantam began to hunt, and once the instinct, that deep-rooted hunting instinct, had been unearthed, Bantam ceased to become the family pet. By eight months he was a remorseless, passionate hunter, a dog who quested from dawn till dusk, a dog who ran himself to a state of exhaustion, paused, and then continued to hunt still further. By dint of Barrister's example, he became steady to rabbits, for Barrister had once received a savage whipping from Kent for his interest in small fry and never forgot the chastisement or the reason for it. He would pass by a crouched bunny, eyeing it cautiously, yearning to chase but conditioned not to. Even when Bantam raced after one, snuffling his presence down a rabbit burrow, snorting like a bellows, Barrister

92

ignored them, and gradually Bantam came to regard the rabbit as unsuitable quarry. It was a rare quality in a hound, this total disregard for coneys, but then Bantam was a warp and weft of rare qualities, as is every good hound.

His hunts with Barrister became longer, more persistent and more successful, but his hunting, his total disregard of anything but the scent of hare and the hunting of the same was to be his undoing in the Probert household. A dozen times and more a police officer from the nearby village had returned him to the anxious family, but next day would find him pursuing new hares, venturing into new country, far from Laurel Green. He was no longer the pet, no longer the surrogate doll to be dressed and made ridiculous in brightly coloured dolls' clothes. He was superbly bred and blood would out. He was a beagle, a small one, but still a hound bred to hunt, to run nose down after his chosen quarry, and such a creature has no place in a pet household. At the end of the year's walk a grateful family returned the tiny hound to Courtney's kennel and retired to Laurel Green with a sigh of relief that the burden of keeping such a dog had been taken off their shoulders. Probert had handed over the hound to Courtney, saying that he realized why beagles were referred to as hounds not dogs. (Dogs, in Probert's eyes, were trainable and biddable pets.) He had then departed.

Courtney was not grateful for the return of the hound. He had hounds enough, saplings in plenty, good-quality stock, level in type and of good conformation, without the ugly little tri-colour. To run him with the pack was to lose uniformity, to make his superb crop of beagles look something of a joke. It was expedient to destroy such an unsightly hound, essential to shoot such an ugly little atavism that not only looked out of place among the superb crop of young saplings in his kennels, but was also a constant reminder that Chorister carried such blood and was capable of producing such offspring again. Courtney had shuddered at the thought of a dozen or so whelps like Bantam appearing in his litters. It was not so easy actually to destroy the quaint little hound, however. The Proberts were his near neighbours, and the daughters constant visitors to the kennels since Bantam had been returned, for the hound now penned up in the yard was incapable of causing havoc and disrupting family life. Restricted as he now was, he had become a revered pet again. The family would certainly not take kindly to the demise of the little oddity. It put Courtney in a bit of a dilemma, and he was grateful when Beddows appeared in the yard to buy any draught hounds Courtney had to spare.

Courtney was more than generous with George. Not only did he like the good-natured, unassuming man, but the fellow's sheer ignorance of beagles and his open admission of his lack of knowledge of the subject did much to endear him to Courtney. Furthermore, most gentlemen who are gentlemen are immediately disarmed by an amateur who innocently states that he will put himself entirely in the gentleman's hands. Few real sportsmen actually enjoy taking candy from a kid. He had literally given Beddows four old stagers who, while they were not top class, were certainly not duffers, and then, as a delicious sort of joke, he had offered Beddows Bantam. Beddows had always bragged that he had seen the potential in the little hound, for as a prize fighter was reputed to be the best person to assess a fighting dog, so a go-getter is often the first to sense the same quality in another. In truth, it was Beddows' ignorance that made him accept the quaint, short-legged, long-coupled little pied hound. It was one of those rare fortuitous mistakes that destiny allows us. Bantam was to become Beddows' most famous hound, a treasure that would dim the greatness of Bantam's illustrious sire and dam, a hound among hounds, in fact. It was a fortunate thing for Beddows that he had accepted Courtney's charity. It was not such a fortunate thing for Lepus.

It was the first time that the Colonel's estate had been hunted by the beagles, for while the old gentleman had allowed various friends of his son to shoot the estate from time to time, the land had been keepered for a number of years and shot by a syndicate, the most influential of which was Courtney; and Courtney had such an interest in beagles that he was able to prevail on the other members of the syndicate not to shoot hares on the estate. Thus the estate had always been well stocked with hares. The number was controlled by poaching and natural wastage, but little else disturbed the equilibrium of the life of the hares on the estate. The persistent hunting of Lepus by men eager to see the little black-striped hare in a show case, a stuffed travesty with glassy eyes and an unnatural stare, had caused a nuisance, but hares are fairly resilient to the onslaught of running dogs.

From time to time Mayhew, a quaint old ex-guardsman, an ex-batman of the Colonel and one who found employment as a game-keeper, had been paid by Courtney to take leverets to restock some country Courtney had found short of hares; but otherwise the hares of the Colonel's estate were relatively unpersecuted. Today all that was to change, however, for the Colonel's nephew – 'The Bugler' as Beddows had jokingly called him – had been made whip to Beddows' pack, and through the youth's influence the estate had been opened for four days of beagling each year. For a season or two it would be an easy spot to hunt, for not only was it free of roads, but hares not used to beagles, not used to the slow but relentless form of hunting, are easily panicked and taken by a pack. A season or so would correct this, but for the moment the hares on the estate were 'green' – ideal quarry for the youngsters in Beddows' pack to test their mettle, quarry which would tax the young hounds, but not too sorely, for it is a curious fact that hares that are impossible for sight hounds to take often fall prey to the slow but sure hunting of beagles.

At one o'clock the meet assembled at the Goat and Compasses, a curious pub, the hanging board of which displayed a huge, naughty-eyed goat, distinctly Priapic, astride a set of dividers; but the pub was not always called by that name. In the days when palmers, hot out of the Holy Land, had walked this place, a religious fever had seized those not equipped to go crusading and houses had been called by holy names. At the spot where the pub now stood had been a hostelry that served as a resting place for pilgrims and which bore a sign stating,

'God Encompasses Us'. Time passed and the Holy Lance, the Grail, the Saracens, were forgotten and the God Encompasses Us became the Goat and Compasses – a spot where trendy county types met and palmers and pilgrims would be decidedly out of place.

A mixed band constituted the meet. Apart from George and his green-clad whips, an odd assortment of folk assembled to follow the hounds on to the virgin pastures of the Colonel's estate. A narcissistic young woman adjusted her head scarf in the mirror of Beddows' Range Rover, striving to get the rustic, wind-blown look. Two young lads, first-time-outers, annoyed the beagles through the trailer slats, while a young social climber, fresh out of the nearby town, lied desperately about his ancestry to two young women who seemed totally uninterested in his tale.

At the door of the Goat is old Hodgekiss who has always been a foot follower of hounds since he was a boy. Hodgekiss is eighty, but Hodgekiss has always been eighty; no one remembers him as any different. He has always been grey-haired, always nut-brown and crinkled, like an ancient walnut. In four years' time he will slide into death slowly, like a senile oak tree taking its time to expire, unhurried in death as in life. The middle-aged man near the green iron railing is Dilks, a useless man, worthless to his wife, a bane upon society, but a prolific breeder who will sire fourteen dirty children, children whom antibodies and home helps will conspire to keep alive in the nasty house in Kimberley Lane, a house that was designed as a slum, and Dilks has helped fulfil the function of the premises. It pleases him to attend a meet, it delights him to pretend not to notice when the cap is passed. He has been prosecuted for poaching the Colonel's land a dozen times. Now he had permission to hunt it, and the idea pleases him. He has no designs on social advancement and will live out his life as a nasty little, sandy-coloured skulker – a snapper-up of unconsidered trifles – spiteful and annoying as a gadfly. Today he will follow, defiant of the fact that the Colonel will be there, glowering at the state of the country that allowed people like Dilks to live. In a few nights he will ferret the banks on Moss Common with a sandy ferret that exactly resembles himself.

That lady talking to Dr Godridge is Kate Nelson, a star's flight apart from Dilks yet united by common bonds. She was the village belle some ten years ago, a pretty, delightful creature, but she spread her charms and favours unwisely and far too well. After a while the *femme fatale* image became a joke and decent men no longer chat to her in the gossip-filled streets of the village. She set her cap at the upper echelon once, but now at thirty-five years of age and ravaged by incessant wear, she considers anyone socially acceptable. She will flutter through her aimless, loveless life like an insipid, fading, autumnal butterfly that has lost its gaudy summer pollen. Now she has turned up at the meet in the faint hope that someone socially acceptable from outside the village will attend. She will be unlucky today. She will be unlucky for the rest of her life. Indeed, it is better to have loved and lost than to have loved and loved and loved.

The tall, distinguished gentleman, aged maybe sixty, standing there talking to and trying to avoid Kate Nelson is Dr Godridge, who somehow or other has landed the post of Hunt Secretary. He seems confused about his position with the hunt, and for the life of him he cannot remember how or when he was elected to the task. He will complete the day with the beagles, partly because it is expected of him, and partly to escape the attentions of the Nelson woman. He looks up and sees George. 'Ah, Beddows,' he utters. 'I'll have a word with you,' but George appears not to hear – he, too, has had problems with the Nelson woman, and does not wish to chance another encounter with her.

That band of scarf-headed ladies babbling over their gin and tonics are local notables, or rather the wives of local notables – the bored wives of local notables, in fact. Overweight through good living and self-indulgence, bored through inactivity, they will run those muddy fields without quite knowing why, returning breathless and mud-speckled to their Rotarian husbands without so much as seeing a hare – a fact for which they are profoundly grateful. They will tramp these fields, climb these stiles, roll sidewards under the ripping, slashing strands of barbed wire, as a sort of social exercise. At the end of the day each will make a silent confession to their innermost souls that they do not approve of blood sports, and don't really like beagles. Next week they will turn out again, though, remarking on how pleasurable the previous week's hunt had been.

The youth standing next to the hound trailer in a hacking-jacket and ridiculous frilled shirt, like an incongruous extra from *Showboat*, is John Coney, a trainee farmer, his employment card says. He grew up in the mining town to the south of the Goat, and his interest in birds and small livestock inspired his parents to push him into farming. He will flounder his way through agricultural school, through acres of cowpats, a far cry from his hamster-filled, guinea pig-festooned terraced house in Hillditch. It is his first meet with the beagles. It will also be his last. He will sense that his dress is wrong, his manners alien, his accent different. Before the end of the day, he will feel rejected, unable to mingle. Next week he will go to the lunchtime disco in the nearest town, only to realize that he will be as out of place there as well.

That knot of seething skirts, of bubbling and boiling blouses, the noisy, rumbustious, quarrelling, squalling group near the long-based Land-Rover is the Proberts, out for the day, to quarrel, exasperate and annoy, and possibly to watch Bantam hunt – that is, if they can still remember Bantam, lost as he is now among hosts of similarly coloured hounds all sired by him, all capable of drawing winces at the Peterborough show. Today the Proberts will flap and flutter across field, bog down in plough, giggling at the increasing thicknesses of clay adhering to their 'specially bought' country boots. They will run with the hounds for an hour, mindless of the field craft beagling requires, after which a quarrel, a calamity, a bout of tearfulness will bring the occasion to an abrupt and irritable end. That man seated there, head across the Land-Rover steering wheel, is Mr Probert. He will be glad when the brood has generated enough strife and noise to abandon the meet. At this moment in time he would rather be at his office desk, attending a business conference, or on a factory floor – anywhere, in fact, away from his petticoat-filled hell.

The lean, angular man standing back from the others is Jim Daniels. He is underkeeper for the Colonel, an unhappy man at this moment in time, eager as Probert to see the day ended. He will be delighted to see his wards depart, for he has been appointed by the Colonel to ensure that not too much havoc takes place, that not too many pheasants are disturbed, not too many fences broken. It is the first time the pack has hunted his estate. With luck it might be the last. He is a dour man of simple needs, and the mixed collection of folk descending on his Eden disturbs him. He will wince each time the beagles flush a hare, for he knows each hare on the shoot, he has watched each leveret grow from infancy, and to see them disturbed by this noisy, bobbery pack of folks and dogs is not to his liking. He has few social pretences. He will deliberately call the hounds dogs and delight at the twisted, displeased faces of the whips.

That man there, stout but strongly built, with two terriers on chains, is Joe Berkeley. A season ago he was terrier man for Beddows, a good terrier man who knew the country, its earths, its pitfalls like no other. He is oddly out of place among the crowd, but then, who is in place? He will make for the high ground knowing the hares will come back that way. He has hunted all his life, earth-stopping when payment was half a crown an earth and five bob deducted for one unstopped that let a fox to ground. For four years he made a sketchy living, but after that there were few five-bob earths. His two terriers are battle-scarred, one has little left of its nose. Today he will lag behind until the Proberts exhaust themselves, for, like his dogs, he dislikes the noise of unruly children. He will be an asset to any hunt, for he knows hunt parlance, hunt protocol and, above all, is a novelty to the field, for he knows hares and hounds.

Altogether they are a curious bunch gathered together to witness a social event, a hint of the countryside, a relic of a better, more leisurely age. They have met to enjoy a social event, and not one of them, Dilks aside, wishes to see the hounds hunt a hare to death – but they will, Bantam will see to that.

At one-twenty precisely, George tapped loose the pegs holding the trailer hatch and the brood spilled out, dashing around the yard of the Goat Inn in gleeful anticipation, voiding faeces and urine in excitement at the prospect of the day's hunting. Bantam, Barrister, Chorister, Choirboy, all scratted the earth of the lawn in a display of masculinity, while a young bitch rolled sycophantically on her back in front of the Probert girls; but it was a short-lived spell of gaiety. Beddows' pack was not famed for its beauty, but the hounds were noted for their grim determination at hare hunting, and in no time they had ceased to be a band of mindless, excited individuals and had coalesced into a hunting pack, a grim, murderous little band, whose merry tails and excited yelping hid savage hearts, unerring noses and a stamina drawn from a passionate desire to slay their quarry.

During their early days, before Beddows understood the technique of handling a foot pack, the beagles had rioted on rabbit, and once in fallow field left the scent of hare to hunt a big dog fox. It had been useless to call them off. They had run the fox unceasingly, with a fervour that would have put a fox-hound pack to shame, finally cornering him and killing him in Duffy's barn. A grim struggle had ensued, for beagles are diminutive hounds, ill-suited to the killing of large quarry, and many still bore the slash marks inflicted by the fox as he made a futile and savage attempt to keep off the sea of biting, boiling, baying hounds. After that season they had jelled into a hare-hunting pack, content to run only one quarry and ignoring the coneys feeding too late and too far from their burrows. They even became oblivious to the heavy scent of fox left on the autumn thistles.

In moments they had united into a team and were moving for the Lodge Gate and on to the country they were to hunt. But with them, in a less orderly manner, moved the 'field' – the Nelson woman still pestering Godridge and the Probert children rioting over the distribution of chocolate bars. On the far side of Lodge Gate they began to cast for scent, each hound seemingly eager to be the first to find. Along the earth path they stopped a moment, almost mouthing some rabbit pellets, fresh, damp and strongly scented, but the scent offered no magic for them and they drifted on, climbing until they reached the stone walls of the high pastures, fields too dry for cattle, but sheep pastures that had once reared stock for the famous Coke of Peterborough, stock twice the size of the scrawny native sheep, scarcely bigger than good-sized hares. At the high pastures in a dingle, the shelter of which allowed nettles to grow tall and rank, they encountered the first scent of the day.

Bellman, a pied son of Bantam, found first, and his eager questing and soft, almost uncertain bay brought the rest of the pack into the hollow where, an hour ago, a hare had sat cropping the tough fescue grass. For a few seconds only there was almost confusion, and then Bantam pushed his way through the ranks of snuffling hounds and took up the line, questing furiously, his long ears almost brushing the grass as he ran. He forged ahead, drinking in the fresh scent, frenzied to find the beast that had left those bitter-scented pellets in the hollow. In no time the rest of the pack were with him, for Bantam was seldom wrong, seldom mistaken, and his judgement was respected by hounds and field alike.

'Look, Bantam is hunting,' Probert had said, nudging his youngest daughter, but her sticky, chocolate-bar-stained hands were engaged in gripping and pulling her squalling sister's hair and she had no interest in the hunt. The spasmodic, yickering bark now became a series of excited, high-pitched yelps as the scent grew stronger.

Further down the hill, on the leeward side of Crooked Oak, a young female hare grazed nervously, plucking the grass. She had been born in the first warm days of the April of that year, and had seen little hunting. She stood there, ears erect, belly full, but anxiety made her crop the grass that had been grazed short by sheep. She knew little of dogs, and only once had some louts with whippets run her that autumn. They had caused her little trouble, and she had left the tiny, greyhound-like dogs standing as soon as she sensed they might take her. For a while the four whippet dogs, who had enough greyhound blood to make them useful as coursers, had pursued her, but she had left them far behind, left them to give tongue as did most of their kind when they saw a quarry escaping. She was a large doe, for she had been sired by the giant jack who had sheltered and fed on the spongy fields near Burnt Cottage Meadow. He, too, had been a powerful beast, weighing eleven pounds in summer fat. Twice had he bested Lepus in the spring rut battles along Common Edge. Twice had he out-fought the seven-pound, lop-eared veteran. But he had proved slower than his small opponent and he had been taken by a rough-coated, stringy lurcher during the first naked days after the corn had been cut.

The men with the lurcher had marvelled at the size of the hare, estimating his weight at sixteen pounds, a weight that had grown a pound before the towels were put on the taps in Tapper's bar. They had eulogized over his size, been staggered over his giant heart and huge hind legs, proclaiming him to be the King of Hares and the dog that took him, as he cat-napped out of the wind in the grass near the Burnt Cottage, a wonder. They had praised the dog, its speed, its sudden snatching at the fleeing hare, and proclaimed it the best hare-killer in Britain. Yet later that day he had also run Lepus, who was smaller, more aware of danger, and not once during the tedious, uneventful course did the dog look like turning, let alone catching the small, black-spined hare. That fact had been forgotten as the men caroused in the bar of Tapper's pub. Now the daughter of the giant hare, a ten-pound doe, grazed nervously, awaiting her first hunt by beagles.

They crossed the rise and came down on her, questing, snuffling, baying as they came. Twice she assumed a half-crouch, hoping to be overlooked by the sea of dogs that converged on her. Twice she contemplated freezing to escape the hounds, but as the baying became louder and the sound of hunting more frenzied, she took flight. Bandbox, a draught hound from a nearby pack, saw her first and gave tongue with a frantic rolling bay. They were on her now, running her by sight, coming at her like the horns of the bull that the Zulus had used to engulf their enemies. She had not quickened her stride, for the hounds posed little threat to her and she was unused to the ways of beagles. At the edge of Lyndey Copse she slipped through the hedge and vanished from the sight of her pursuers. They soon arrived at the hedge, however, still babbling at the disappearance of the hare. Twice they ran the line up and down the hedge until Bantam found the gap through which she had disappeared. He pushed through the gap, widening it, almost oblivious to the hurt caused him by thorn and wire, and the pack followed. Choirboy, aptly named, gave a falsetto squeak. They had found her again.

She turned now, running back uphill to the maze of drystone walls, exactly as Joe Berkeley had said she would, pausing every now and then as if to determine whether she was still being pursued. The oncoming cacophony of snuffles and bays, of frantic footfall, left her in no doubt that she was. At the edge of the first field she paused in her flight and, with a sudden leap, half-cleared, half-scrambled the dry sandstone wall like a tiny chamois. Uphill she ran towards the field, almost ignoring the crowd, totally occupied by the pursuing hounds. A shout from a tearful Probert child checked her and she paused on the horns of a dilemma, as if trying to decide whether to flank the field or to turn downhill towards the hounds. She stood there, every muscle aquiver, poised ready for flight, her eyes black and prominent, her giant ears erect, assessing every sound, interpreting every bark. Berkeley slowly reached into his pocket and took out his handkerchief, holding it high with a gentle, unhurried movement, signalling her presence to Beddows and the pack, but there was no need for the gesture.

At the drystone wall the pack had checked, puzzled by the disappearance of the hare and the absence of scent. For a while they had padded around nervously, baffled by the scentless ground, until Bantam found again, nosing the drystone wall, licking the tiny patch of urine that the hare had voided as she had scaled the stones. He leaped upwards twice, his tiny legs unable to propel his body over the wall, but on the third attempt his feet gripped the stone, and he levered himself over the wall. The pack followed rapidly. Bantam was rarely wrong. The sound of baying became louder and the doe, still mesmerized by the field, contemplated running around the crowd of people who stood there silently – Proberts excepted – awaiting her decision. But the infinitely small movement of Berkeley's arm, the fluttering of the handkerchief decided her. She turned back almost into the thick of the hounds, leaping at right-angles to avoid their rush, but as she leaped a youngster, or maybe an old hound, struck at her and chopped her in mid-flight. She was down now, still alive, but the mêlée of hounds converged on her, silencing her almost ghostly scream, tearing her, ripping her, killing her instantly and then pulling and plucking her body to pieces.

The field converged on the kill, but there was little left to see or hear save for some sparse tufts of hair that blew across the meadow, pieces that were pursued by a hound still young enough to indulge in such foolishness. George groaned. Above the pack the Bugler was blasting forth his victory carollade, raucously, tunelessly, excessively. Dilks was drooling somewhat, for he had seen the kill clearly and had been excited by the sudden futile sidewards leap of the doe. Death and pain always excited Dilks, while the Nelson woman had cornered Doctor Godridge again. Berkeley replaced his white handkerchief and shook his head, turning slightly so as not to watch the Probert girls, who were fighting again. In the thick of the mêlée of hounds, Bantam had paused to lick a spot of blood and wolf down the tiny blobs of half-digested grass and twigs that had been voided through the torn stomach of the hare. Interest in the kill diminished, and Beddows lifted the pack towards the old orchard near Burnt Cottage.

It was a quiet spot, a good place for hares to feed, a place where the disturbing feet of sheep and cattle rarely trod. It was a sheltered spot where ancient varieties of apple and pear still fruited on the moss-covered, unpruned trees. It was a place often frequented by hares, a place where Lepus, unaware of the furious bloody kill near the drystone walls, was feeding. He was older than the doe, more aware of the dangers that dogs presented, but, like her, he was a newcomer to beagling, ignorant of the inexorable nature of the stunted hounds. Within minutes he was to be well educated.

Whip curled, Beddows led the way towards the old orchard. The place had a curious history. A century ago, Morgans, an articulate, choleric Welshman, had resigned from his post at Oxford during one of his frequent bouts of melancholia and come to live in the old cottage. He had been a baffling enigma to the villagers, this blustering, outspoken man, whose soft tongue and brittle comments contrasted sharply with his drunken bouts and temper tantrums. For a while the villagers had referred to him, half derogatively, half respectfully, as 'Schooly', but the bouts of Saturday-night drunkenness and his wild singing in a language they could not understand, coupled with his fiery temper and prowess with his fists, had made them wary of him. Thus he had lived out his blaspheming, foul-mouthed days in isolation, walking to the village each week to drink and brawl, fermenting the apples and pears into coarse, unpalatable, acidic cider and perry to drink during week days. The vicar had referred to him as the Antichrist during a sermon designed as a tirade against the ungodly in the village, and the title had pleased Morgans, who had rejected the puritanic life imposed by his Chapel-bred parents, and the sermon incited him to further deeds of godlessness. Sober, he was more than a match for the vicar – timid and cosy as the curates of *Punch* – and drunk, he was a fearsome creature.

Thus, for twenty years, Morgans lived in the old cottage, dying eventually of cirrhosis of the liver, expiring in filth and blasphemy, unloved and a long way from home. No one had come to live in the cottage after that, partly because of its inaccessible nature and its poor well that ran dry every summer, and partly because of the memory of the dissolute Welshman and the stories of his drunken fury. After a while, rain and snow destroyed the roof and the furniture rotted away. Children pillaged the sodden, leather-bound volumes of Herodotus and Pliny and used the pages for fires – fires that eventually consumed the rotting, derelict cottage. Now fireweed, the flaming, rosebay willow herb, grew where Morgans had preached his drunken, blasphemous sermons to his dogs and cats, and Lepus browsed on groundsel where Morgans had fought a bloody battle with two of Tapper's great-uncles after a transient but fertile affair with their sister.

104

At the edge of the orchard, near the ruins of the crumbling drystone wall, Bantam stopped and sniffed up the rank sweetness of the fresh urine of a hare. He cast about wildly – wildly, that is, unless one knew the real nature of his actions. His enthusiasm was almost a controlled enthusiasm, as if he doubted his first opinion of the freshness of a scent and would not speak until he had appraised the situation carefully. Godridge had once said it was difficult not to credit Bantam with human intelligence, and then, glancing up at Dilks' broken, brown teeth, he had shaken his head as if to dispel such a thought. Bantam dwelled on the scent for a full three seconds, and then he spoke.

In the overgrown orchard, shielded by a clump of dead and withered thistles, Lepus stood – one ear erect, the other, damaged by Kemp's hawk, protruding at a jaunty angle. All barking meant danger, even the yap of a ridiculous woman's woolly lap-dog could mean hurt. He knew well enough. He had not survived these six years in a hostile, brutal world without regarding dogs and men with fear. At the first bay he chinned a clump of dried grass and prepared to amble off to the open fields. Once he crouched, an instinctive posture that had protected his kind over a million years, but something deeper, a sense more primeval than instinct, made him aware that crouching would avail him nothing against this foe. He ambled quietly through the tangle of fireweed and bramble towards a gap in the wall, beyond which lay the open fields where his lightning burst of speed could be best utilized. It was at that moment, as he stood upon the ruined drystone wall, that all hell broke loose in the tangle which had once been an orchard. Bantam had scented him and was in hot pursuit, running the strong, clean scent through the weedy bramble patch. Lepus loped away to the open fields, stopping a moment and regarding the assembled field with an amazed, terrified stare. Godridge slowly raised his handkerchief, while Probert stifled a war whoop from his youngest harridan.

Lepus stood amazed, alarmed, almost petrified by the crowd of people silently awaiting his next move. Behind him, Bantam, Bellman and Bandbox had clambered the wall, scarcely thirty yards from the motionless hare. Lepus flashed into flight downhill away from the cottage and its decaying orchard, the hounds in hot pursuit, baying almost hysterically now they had sighted the quarry.

Dilks edged nearer to the Probert woman, still comely in spite of her spate of breeding and rearing her brood. 'They'll 'ave 'im now. 'Is legs is long in the back, so he's quick up'ill an' slow down.' She smiled, trying not to breathe lest she should inhale his tobacco-reeking breath and musky body odour.

Berkeley shook his head and uttered under his breath, 'Christ, where does the idiot get these tales? He should be bloody locked up.'

Lepus paused at the hedge in the water meadow and sniffed. The fear scent of the doe still hung around the spot, masked by the foul, terrifying scent of hound. While the baying behind him grew louder, he stopped as if intimidated, made wary by the scent of the now dead hare. There was little time for contemplation, however, and he flashed through the gap, gathering speed, losing the pack and finally coming to rest in a patch of alder near to the river's edge. He stopped a while, ear still erect, chinning the crenellated bark of the alder stems, restless even at rest, alert to every danger. Behind him the baying was faint. Somewhere, possibly as he had leaped Cotman's Brook, splashing up a tiny storm of grit in the fast-flowing waters, he had lost them, and even now they quested up and down the bank of the stream to rediscover his delicious, fear-filled odour.

He crouched, ears to back, regaining his breath for the next danger that would manifest itself in his peril-filled life. There was little prospect of waiting. The baying had become louder again. Bantam had leaped the narrow stream and found the scent, and the others splashed joyfully after him. As they neared the alder beds, another hare, an adult jack, leaped up scarcely twelve yards from the approaching pack, and temporarily the hounds split into two questing groups. George and his Bugler coaxed them back. Bantam was hunting a different scent and Bantam was always right.

Within thirty yards of the alder clump, the baying increased in intensity and Lepus exploded into flight once more. Barrister saw him and let loose almost a whoop in excitement, a strangled cry, a hybrid between a bark and a bray. Again they were on him, running by sight again, spreading out like a trawler's net to entrap the fleeing hare. He skirted the damp river's edge, unable to lose his pursuers, for the damp grass held his scent like a sponge. They were two hundred yards behind him as he reached the river bridge and turned uphill once more, dashing through the neat, well-kept hedge and racing to the drystone walls again.

Dilks watched him come, leering at the comely Mrs Probert. 'Watch 'im now. Those long legs'll take 'im up'ill quicker than down.' She smiled back at him warily. She was up-wind now, and his stench was less offensive.

At the drystone wall Lepus paused and ran along the sunken land downhill from it. At last he stopped, faltered, and leaped the wall, now in full view of the field. A half-dozen handkerchiefs appeared on the skyline as Lepus doubled back to run alongside the sheep tracks at the foot of the wall. He panicked and slunk out into the field towards a flock of sheep – sheep that he normally avoided lest their sharp little hooves should trample him as he lay at rest in his hastily constructed form. He loped through the flock and stopped, panting loudly. Bantam had found the spot where Lepus had leaped the wall and the pack cascaded over the stonework, toppling flat slivers of sandstone from the top.

They quested a moment or so, drinking in his scent at the point where he had run along the sheep track, his odour less strong now that it was mingled with the scent of sheep. Chorister stopped and sniffed at the point where the hare had left the track, and Bantam confirmed the hound's opinion.

Beddows groaned aloud, 'Christ, if the Proberts yell we'll have a stampede on our hands,' but the sheep moved quietly left of the approaching hounds, who once more viewed the now fleeing shape of Lepus. They were on him again, and for the first time in his life he experienced the awful weariness that had brought so many hares into the jaws of beagles. He ran, unable to shake off the slow, wilful, unyielding pack of hounds. He was still fast enough to outpace the fastest beagle, still with enough stamina to escape them in a lengthy run, but while his stamina began to wane, theirs became stronger by the minute. He turned back into the old orchard, but the scent of hound and trampled fireweed stalks deterred him from entering the spot. Again he turned downhill, the orchard shielding him from the view of the field.

For a while he crouched, panting, in a hollow a hundred yards from the orchard wall. He was tired now and his lungs were hot and fiery. Each step, each bound, each breath was an effort, an almost gargantuan effort. 'Fear lends wings to the hunted hart,' the poet had said, but fear, even the most blind terror, can only tap the adrenalin-induced speed for so long, after which the beast is left with a weak and empty feeling and is resigned to death. The ancients had said that when stamina is depleted, drained to its limits, only the *hochma* – the vital, life-creating, primeval force that walked upon the waters at the dawn of time – propels a hunted beast on, and Lepus had drawn on the well of stamina for an hour now. The sound of the field moving to position themselves for the hunt disturbed him, and he loped away, exhausted almost to the point where he would accept death, the fearful ripping, the dreadful mangling of his limbs. As he neared the ancient oak gate, however, he met a hound who had strayed from the pack in the water meadow and was trying to rejoin the hunt. It saw him and he turned, running uphill again. Berkeley raised his hand-kerchief once more.

The hound ran him hard. He had little difficulty in avoiding it, but it taxed his energy still further, draining every muscle, every fibre of his being, and when Bantam and his ravenous brood cleared the rise, skirting the orchard wall, he had little left to give. They saw him, ran him by sight, and he side-stepped the straying hound, heading for the gate again. He reached it with the pack a mere twenty yards behind, and gained somewhat as the pack struggled through the narrow gaps in the oak structure. Lepus redoubled his efforts, somehow aware that the baying, screaming horde was gaining strength from his weakness. He reached the wall again and leaped to clear it. It was an easy jump, one he had made a hundred times – and at his best, fresh and unwinded, he would have scarcely regarded the wall as an obstacle. He was not at his best, however, with his head a mass of swirling, painful fog, his limbs weighted with lead. He leaped, touched the top of the drystone wall and fell back again. He glanced around. The pack bore down on him inexorably, driving him to greater efforts. Once more he attempted the jump, once more he crashed to the ground, his limbs too heavy to co-ordinate a jump. On the third attempt he made the top of the wall with his tiny front legs and levered his body and hind legs to the topmost stones. He literally toppled to the ground and ran slowly, lack-lustrely, to the alder bushes. There was no strength left now, and his mind anaesthetized his body, making its fate more acceptable. He splashed through the brook once more, and limped into the alder grove near the river's edge.

Bantam cleared the wall at his second leap, losing only seconds by his first failure. At the far side of the wall he quested madly, aware that the different odour emitted by the prey meant that it was close to exhaustion, ready for the taking. He had smelled such scent a hundred times or more, and the change of odour made him redouble his efforts. He hunted madly until he found the trail again, running it rapidly now, babbling as he did so, inspiring his fellow Furies to greater efforts and greater noise. He splashed through the brook, the water soaking his hide and that of his fellow hounds, making him lose the scent a moment or so. But it was a temporary respite, a brief breathing-space for Lepus. In seconds they had found the trail again, and were running eagerly towards the alder grove, to the spot where Lepus crouched, the last of his energy now dissipated. Field, Master, whips, were all far behind, and the hunt had degenerated into a private duel 'twixt Lepus and the pack. Near the alder grove, Bantam forged ahead, his frenzy compensating for his shortness of limb; and by the time he sighted Lepus, only Bandbox and a young green hound were with him. He bore down on Lepus like death itself.

Bantam crashed through the rank bog grass towards the spot where the exhausted hare crouched, awaiting the inevitable. Bantam was on him in a trice, striking at the downed, spent hare, who rose instinctively, throwing himself sidewards to avoid the bite. Twice Bantam struck and twice Lepus evaded the bite with a bound, for he was too weak to run. On the third onslaught, Bantam, now aided and abetted by the unentered hound, lunged for Lepus, who leaped through the alder branches, crashing down into the fast-flowing river, while Bantam ran as if berserk to find a gap in the alder tangle, to swim after the escaping hare. The plunge into the icy waters winded Lepus, but the suddenness of the submersion, the final stage of fright, drew upon the spirit force that lurked within the hare. Instinctively he began to swim for the far bank.

Beddows arrived shortly afterwards to find Bantam swimming after the hare into the middle of the river. He blew to recall the hound, patting the youngster as he did so. 'Where my poor trembling hound feared to follow,' he laughed. It was the only poetry he knew – Longfellow's 'Skeleton in Armour', a poem learned as punishment for sloth.

He laughed and remembered Mr Frobisher, the irate English teacher in his secondary-modern school. 'You'll never make anything in this world, George, you're just a born loser.'

Bantam regained the bank, shaking his pied skin to shed the water and mud. 'Damn nigh had him then, old man, and I'd have let you take him except we're not welcome on the other side. Pity,' he said, stroking the wet and weary hound. 'A pity, he gave us a hell of a run.' He turned and rejoined the field.

Lepus climbed wearily out of the icy water and shook his thin coat, wagging his head at odd angles to clear the water from his damaged ear. He climbed the bank stiffly, falling back onto the pebbles twice, but within the hour he was browsing again and had forgotten the dreadful hunt. Thus Lepus returned to the fields that had seen his birth. He had come home, so to speak, but there could be no place that was not thwart with danger for him.

'D'you know, Brennan, you're besotted with that bloody dog, out of your mind with it. Never seen a man, even in the tribe, so dog daft as you.'

Brennan yawned, ignoring Harvey, and continued to stroke Czar's silky ears. It was a habit more than a caress, but Brennan found Harvey's interest in his fondling of the dog amusing.

'Swear to God, I do, that you think more of the beast than you did of Liz.'

Harvey could have bitten off his tongue at the response to his idle comment, for he saw Brennan wince at the barb. Liz had been Brennan's greatest love – his only love, perhaps, for someone as intense as Brennan gives himself only once in a lifetime, after which there is no more to give. He had been bedazzled by the tiny woman, neat and elfin-like, and amazed that a girl some thirteen years his junior would up and leave her comfortable home, her husband and children, to live in his solitary, ugly cottage. He had been fond of her, had given her what he had, but his philandering, his sexual adventures, indulged in to prove that his fading virility didn't prevent him acquiring women, had driven her away. He had been drunk for a month afterwards, and during one of his bouts of melancholy had told Harvey that the feeling for Liz had been infatuation.

'Infatuation means made foolish, Harvey. That's what the bitch has done to me. Made me foolish. Christ, no, Harvey, I'm a self-made man. I've always been foolish.' That morning he had read a poem aloud to a bored and indifferent 3C, '*Mais ou sont les neiges d'antan?* Where are the last year's snows?' He had been unable to explain to the class, but he knew exactly what Villon had meant. Now, at forty-six years old, ravaged by bad food, his mind etched with bitterness, he would never find happiness again. He consoled himself by saying, 'Well, you old sod, you had two good years, and how many other bastards can boast even that?'

He shook his head sadly, ignoring the gypsy. He sighed a long, deep sigh and continued to stroke Czar's feathered ears, staring without seeing into the flickering flames of the fire. During the last few months he had become increasingly pensive, aware of his own loneliness, his lack of achievement. A year from now his sense of failure, his inability to communicate with his fellow men, and his awful loneliness would combine to push him over the slender *arrête* of sanity. He already felt persecuted by all and sundry, resentful of anyone who was successful, bitter at anyone who disturbed his solitude, even though he welcomed any intrusion into his quiet, miserable, empty life. Three weeks previously his phone had rung incessantly one evening: small unimportant messages, tiny almost irrelevant matters – the sort that clutter the lives of most folk. For a while he tolerated the ringing, even finding pleasure in the fact that such attention must mean that he was relatively popular, but as the evening progressed, he stared harder, more intently into the fire, seeing arrogant, unlovely, critical faces in the flames. He had been irritated by the ringing sound, the silly voice of the last caller, perhaps, and finally, in a bout of rage, he had smashed the phone, noting at the time that the death agonies of the machine resembled those of a dying child.

Harvey had remarked on the damage next day.

'It kept bloody ringing,' Brennan had said defensively.

'Ye could have taken it off the hook,' Harvey had whispered, but he knew Brennan's problems were deeper and more acute than the fact that he found the phone annoying. He was becoming remote, distant, even with Harvey, and the old man found it increasingly difficult to tolerate Brennan's irrational moods and tempers. To Harvey, used as he was to whatever the day might bring, accepting all things stoically in his never-hurrying, never-worrying manner, Brennan's paranoia was baffling. He had seen eccentrics before, watched loneliness push the person who was 'different' into a state of lunacy, until they became as irrational, illogical as Ben Gunn. His wife had skivvied for Mister Peters, a quiet, doddery old man – a bachelor, celibate and neat as a spinster. And he had seen the old man slip into premature senility because no one cared about him.

'You need another woman, Brennan. Someone to keep the place alive, maybe just to talk to, to break the loneliness of the night-time.'

'She'd have little chance to get a bloody word in edgeways, what with you chuntering on like a bloody old woman yourself,' Brennan had spat back, silencing the Romany.

A year ago Brennan would have regretted saying this, and have been sorry for his acidic tongue that functioned almost independently of his mind. Now he was stung to fury by Harvey's intrusion in his personal life. 'Old bastard!' he muttered, staring into the fire.

Harvey desperately sought to change the subject. 'Seen your hare on the water meadows this morning. Reckon he must have swum the river. Summat pushed him to do so, for hares won't swim unless they're frit.'

'Frightened, not frit, you bloody old fool,' Brennan thought, but he replied, 'Probably another, Harvey, son or grandson maybe, with the same markings. He must have sired a hundred in the last few years.'

'No,' said Harvey, warming to the subject, noting that Brennan had abandoned his melancholic fire-staring. 'No, it's the same. A small jack with a black stripe. One of his ears askew – fight maybe, or injury. Must be six years or more now. Old for a hare.'

'They live to twelve or more,' said Brennan pompously, always the teacher in and out of school.

'Aye, twelve,' Harvey replied. 'But folks who said such things kept them in walled gardens where nothing could 'arm them and nobody could do them 'urt.'

Brennan looked up sharply. 'How in hell did you know that, Harve?' He was always surprised when Harvey came out with these tiny pieces of wisdom, pearls that he had gleaned from some place or other during his long and interesting life. Nothing was wasted in his squirrel existence, and he hoarded unnecessary things until his yard and mind became a rubbish dump filled with curious bric-à-brac. Brennan had taught him to read fifteen years before, and now he read avidly, voraciously, not heeding what he absorbed.

'I read sometimes, Brennan. Can read, you know. But I tell you he's back on the water meadows, near Vickery's. Saw 'im there yesterday, grazing on sow thistle on the old plough. Same hare, Brennan. I know him. Some beast, surviving six years in a place where all want to race 'im to death. Bet he's the King of Hares, Brennan. The King of Hares,' he repeated, pleased with the phrase he had concocted.

'Bullshit, Harvey! Hares don't have kings. The sod has just had a good run of luck, that's all. Maybe he's learned to keep out of the way of dogs. Maybe there's a shortage of foxes or whatever on the land where he's been living.'

'Not true, Brennan,' Harvey chimed excitedly. 'Talk at Tapper's place says he's been run damned near to death on the Colonel's estate, pushed by whippets, greyhounds, long dogs, the lot. All folks have run him – Romanies, poachers, hedge wumpers, the lot. He's beaten everything. Tapper said the beagles pushed a hare across the river only last month – could have been 'im. They say it ran nearly all the hounds into the soil before he took to water. The King of Hares, that, all right.'

'You're a born romantic, Harvey, and a born bloody dreamer. A hare's a hare. I had bad luck with the old bitch, sheer bad luck, and now this silly talk's gone to your bloody empty head. Tomorrow, if you like. Come tomorrow at dawn, and I'll show you the King of Hares in action. Pound to a penny Czar takes him. Pound to a penny this time tomorrow you'll be stewing him.'

'Meat for a cat,' Harvey spat. 'He's tough old meat. Bet he creaks when he runs.'

'Then he'll be the easier for taking, Harvey. Czar will take him tomorrow. Turn up at dawn and you'll carry him home. Won't he, Czar?' he murmured, lovingly stroking the dog's tasselled ears.

Czar looked up almost knowingly. His facial expression had favoured the collie and his eyes were intelligent, a far cry from the blank, unintelligent eyes of the greyhound that had sired him. He had served Brennan well, bringing the bitter man the only degree of fame and success he would ever know. He had been run lightly as a puppy, allowed to chase and snap up early- and late-feeding rabbits a few yards from their burrows. They had been pointless runs, most of the time, for the dog had no chance of taking the ever-alert rabbits, but the experience had taught him much. He learned to anticipate, to understand the ways of the quarry. He learned which quarry was takeable and which would be wasted effort. Above all, he learned to run cunning, to turn the scampering bunnies off the hedgerow, pushing them off their usual well-padded runs on to paths with which they were unfamiliar.

Lurching, Harvey had called the skill, and, though he boasted that his father had a better beast, Harvey knew Czar was a world beater. The dog would walk quietly through the summer pastures, silent as a cat, stealthy as a pointer, marking the crouched partridges and striking at them as they rose in the air, their noisy wing-beat designed to deflect a blow from an attacking predator. He had been slow to learn the technique of taking them, alarmed by their noisy, whirling flight, but six months later he would strike left and right at the exploding covey, laying low two and sometimes three partridges. 'Christ, he's a real lurcher,' Harvey had said, the ultimate accolade from one who boasted that his tribe had lived by the sagacity of their lurchers. Czar, however, was eighteen months old, a picture of strength and beauty, before he saw his first hare.

Brennan had been visiting the Mellish woman, as Harvey called her – a quiet, dowdy divorcee who lived 'top side' of Cotters End. She was unlovely and boring, more concerned with the amount of meat on the local Chinese restaurant's spare ribs than with Brennan's gift for words. He had visited her out of boredom, or maybe because he could exercise his spite by making a quick and easy conquest. He could never fathom out which. So, dog at heel, he tramped the three miles through Dwyer's Woods to the Mellish woman's house, ostensibly for his evening meal. He had half-vaulted, half-climbed the mossy stile by Lowrie's cornfield when he saw the hare, a young jack still the right side of winter – a fair and testing course for a sapling. He touched the dog and held it close to his side as he walked towards the jack. It was foolish to allow a sporting slip, to allow the beast law, for the dog was a puppy and needed early success if it was to become a good hunter of hares.

He edged near the beast, the long silky ears of the dog rustling against his corduroy trousers. Thirty yards now, and then the hare noticed the stalking pair and sprinted away. Czar had exploded into pursuit, his giant strides eating up the distance between the two. In seconds he was over it, reaching his long, drake-like neck down to snap it up. It had jinked and he missed by a foot, but he was on it again, overtaking it as it tried to double back to Dwyer's Woods. Brennan had watched, mesmerized, aghast at the spectacle, as he was at each and every run he ever witnessed. Three times Czar struck, three times he missed, but on the fourth strike Brennan saw him disappear in the long grass, rolling over as if stricken. He had raced up and found the dog, hare in mouth, panting hard but still holding the squealing, struggling quarry. He had turned for home, hare in hand, and made himself drunk on the parsley wine old Mrs Harrison had given him to ward off the flu.

It had been the first of many hares, and Brennan had spent his winter weekends in Norfolk, running the lazy marsh hares through the flat, hedgeless land criss-crossed with dykes. It had been easy running for the dog, and as the winter waxed into spring, Czar had become a good, reliable hare-catcher. The following autumn he improved still further, and by the spring Brennan was plagued with itinerants eager to buy the golden-fawn silky dog. At Thetford Czar had outcoursed a greyhound, killing all three hares during the contest. At Thuxton, Brennan had, against his better judgement, run the dog against two tinker dogs, pied and oil-stained but no newcomers to the marsh-bred hares. Both these he had beaten, and Brennan had lied about the whereabouts of his cottage to the tinkers, for he knew he would get little peace once they knew where he lived. That summer when Harvey and he had visited Appleby Fair, a dozen travelling men had offered him lorries and cars for the golden dog, and bids of a thousand pounds were common that day. Czar was now an idol, a golden, lovely mirror in front of which Brennan could stand and bask in reflected glory. A dozen bitches were brought to him, but Brennan refused to allow him to mate – cautious lest the folk who brought these bitches might visit him again and take the 'Golden Dog'. Czar improved daily. His greyhound blood gave him speed, but the collie sagacity gave him what Harvey called 'canny', the ability to predict the bobbing and weaving of the hare, the gift of somehow knowing where the quarry would turn. Furthermore, his stamina seemed bottomless, and at the end of a mighty, lengthy course he would pant a while and in minutes be ready to run again.

All in all, he would have been a match for Lepus even at the hare's prime, even when the hare had run the tinker's greyhound to death. Now that Lepus was old, Czar was more than a match for the tiny, black-striped hare. The next day promised to be a battle of the giants: the legendary, lop-eared hare, victor of a thousand courses, against the Golden Dog. Four years before it would have been an even contest. Now the odds were decidedly in Czar's favour.

Harvey rose before the birds and walked down the muddy lane towards Brennan's cottage. He slipped the catch, walked inside and boiled water for the black, liver-destroying tea favoured by Brennan. A half-hour later Brennan arose, sullenly, silently, and began to stroke the silken ears of Czar and gaze into the fire Harvey had just lit. He stared silently for twenty minutes, motionless except for his fingers, which twitched as he held the mug of tea, while Harvey rambled on about nothing in particular, embarrassed by Brennan's stony silence. Brennan drank the black, bitter tea and began to rub the side of his face – an odd gesture he had acquired in the last few months, and practised so often that the side of his face was inflamed.

'This is like old times, Brennan, hunting in the dawn light. Like old times.'

'Is it, Harve?' Brennan continued to stare into the dancing flames. 'Nothing is the same, Harvey. All things change, and always for the worse.'

'Now, I dunno, Brennan,' Harvey continued.

But he was silenced by Brennan's cryptic, 'I bloody well do.'

The older man tactfully changed the subject. He gazed through the window at the night rolling back from the fields of Cotters End. 'There's mist s'morning, Brennan. The ground's like thistle down. Doubt if you'll see the little hare in this.'

Brennan continued to rub his face and gaze into the fire. He peered into the flickering redness and saw happier times, times when folk regarded him as a protégé, an academic of sorts, a time when he had little money and even fewer worries. As usual, his thoughts turned to Liz, as they had each and every morning of his empty, pointless life. She was married now, wed to a youth four years her junior and living four miles from Cotters End. He never saw her these days, and would drive eight miles out of his way rather than face meeting her in the streets of the market town. He was only faintly aware of Harvey droning on about the mists, and the sound of Czar drinking the dregs of his tea, splashing, sucking, eating even the tea leaves, licking the wetness from the sides of the stained cup.

'Mist is bad here. It'll be worse on the water meadows,' Harvey droned on.

'Patches. It's only in patches. On the high ground, where the little bastard will feed, there'll be no mist. Czar will take him in one field,

Harvey. A fair slip and the hare's dead.'

Harvey had watched the odd and unhappy man put on his anorak with an old, almost rheumatic jerkiness and made a mental note that Brennan was ageing rapidly. The night before he had urged Brennan to take another woman, one who would make the stark house into a home, but, watching Brennan mumbling to himself and rubbing the side of his face, Harvey now realized that there was no woman who would be able to penetrate the hard shell Brennan had built around himself, no woman who would be able to tolerate the morbid, bitter world in which Brennan had come to live.

They slid through the front gate into the mist, a fine, icy mist that seemed to creep inside their clothes and crystallize on their hair.

'Too much mist, Brennan. The dog'll not be able to see to run.'

'It's in pockets, Harvey. The high ground will be clear.'

They passed Vickery's foetid little hovel, climbed the gate and stood in the meadow pasture. The ground was covered in a layer of cotton wool, a vapour that seemed to swirl with every gust, now revealing gaunt winter thistles, now swallowing them up.

'And the rough places shall be made plain,' Brennan muttered to himself, noting that the mist had given the fields almost a flat, billiard-table look.

'S'get home, Brennan. This fog's no good.'

'Go if you wish, Harve. I'm after the little hare.'

'Dunner be crazy, Brennan. You'll not see a bloody thing.'

But Brennan ignored him and began to climb the gentle slope to the upper pastures. He fumbled for the gate in the dense pocket of fog that covered Harpers Edge, and the old, oak-made structure creaked open. They walked up the slightly steep rise to the field, and dog and men surveyed the upper pastures. Apart from a few hollows, the field was clear of the icy mist.

Brennan brushed the ice crystals from his hair. 'See what I mean, Harvey? Told you.'

'Let's get home, Brennan. I've bad feelings about this place.'

Brennan laughed a mirthless laugh. 'You're like an old woman, Harvey. Full of follies and fantasies and witchcraft.'

'It's not that, Brennan,' the older man almost whined. 'It's a bad place to run. The ground's full of pockets of fog. It'll trip a dog, bring him down, wind him.'

A hare passed in front of them with a slow methodical motion, heedless of the men and the dog. It paused to watch them a moment. Brennan reached down and touched the slip on the straining, whining Czar.

117

'Run him, Brennan, and you'll have the dog tuckered out before the real one.'

Brennan's hand returned, leaving the dog still tugging to be after the fleeing hare.

Far off in the middle of the upper pastures, Lepus, his fur still damp with the mist, crouched shivering in his form. The hare had fed badly during the month since his swim across the icy river. He was no longer a native of this bank, and other hares were hostile to strangers. Lepus no longer remembered these fields – the hollows, the dips, the hedges, the fences where he could throw off a pursuing hound; the wire where he could bring a fast and heavy dog to grief. The tangle at Vickery's was inside the range of another jack, a stronger, more powerful beast who had displayed hostility to Lepus when he had strayed too near to feed on the frozen swedes in Vickery's four-acre field. Here, on the no-man's-land of the upper pastures, he was unpersecuted. No hare claimed these dry fields as its own, and a host of wanderers, hares like himself, off country and uncertain, fed on them. On such land there was cause to be nervous, and he crouched fearfully in a tuft of grass just outside the pool of mist that filled the big hollow in the centre of the upland pasture. A stranger in a strange land, he knew few of the runs that criss-crossed the pastures, each one leading to a gap in the hedge or low places in the drystone walls at the upper end of the field. He crouched nervously, twitching in his form.

His weight was at its lowest now. Not only had the winter been a harsh, frosty and inclement one, but his meal of frozen swedes, snatched nervously from the edge of Vickery's field, had scoured his body, leaving his bowels capable of retaining only dry grass. His run against the beagles, and the sudden dip into the icy river, would not have ruffled a younger beast, but now, poised as he was on the brink of senility, his buck teeth long, broken and yellow, any change in his day-to-day life affected him adversely. He no longer passed coprophagous pellets, and his droppings were foetid and liquid. Millais had given the life expectancy of a hare as twelve years, but this was, as Harvey had said, a figure gleaned from those who had kept hares in enclosed gardens, havens of peace where the only enemy a hare knew was neurosis from confinement within high brick walls. Now, at six years old, he was scarred, his fur tatty like a jumble-sale fur coat, his teeth yellow and brittle. Life had been unkind to him. He had been pursued since birth, harried mercilessly by men, birds and dogs. He was old now, old and tired, old and decrepit. It would be a bad time to meet Czar. He shuffled slightly to gain some little comfort from the frozen form, his torn ear held at an angle like an old man's hearing-

118

trumpet for any sounds wafting up from the lower pastures.

Brennan walked across the fields towards the crouched, now invisible hare, skirting the patches of mist that hung thick and damp within the hollows. Harvey, two paces behind, constantly advised on how wrong it would be to run the dog in these conditions. Of late there had been a rift between the two. It was not a rift caused by anything as positive as a quarrel, but a slow drift away from one another, for Brennan now found Harvey's tales of Romany life irritating. Five years ago, he had enjoyed the yarns, the strange combination of acute observation and folklore that Harvey had spun into tales. Now the mention of Harvey's half-true life in the vardo set Brennan's teeth on edge and filled him with such rage that he became physically ill. He ignored Harvey these days, and Harvey, who in his own quiet way needed an audience for his curious and sometimes ridiculous tales, found this shutting-off distressing.

The dog tugged slightly at the slip, and Brennan stopped, freezing to immobility. Sixty yards away he saw movement in the grass – the flicker of a rump, the twitch of an ear? He was uncertain which, but he was in no doubt that it was the movement of a hare.

He signalled Harvey to slow down and began to stalk the crouched creature. 'It is the black-spined little sod,' he whispered to Harvey as he watched Lepus crouch even lower in the form. 'Right, Harvey, we'll show you the King of Hares. If Czar turns him, he'll kill him, and for any price you care to name.'

Harvey shook his head. Ten years ago or less, Brennan had hunted for the pot, thinning down game only when he needed meat for his dogs or ferrets. Now the death of a beast had become an event on which he would gamble, a vice he despised in the ever-present bands of tinkers that haunted Cotters End. Brennan began to circle the hare to obtain a more satisfactory slip. A slip 'twixt the hedge and the crouched hare would be advantageous, he thought, though Czar found hedges no obstacle. The dog tugged slightly at the slip and whined softly. He could no longer see the crouched hare, but the excitement racing down the slip from Brennan, the sound of Brennan's breath coming as a hiss, told him it was almost time to be released. Czar tugged slightly at the slip, and at that moment Lepus chose to run. The animals leaped into motion almost at the same instant. The final duel had begun.

Lepus had watched the approaching pair for a minute or so, trying to gauge whether he had been seen, whether they would pass him by unnoticed. He eyed the dog suspiciously. It worried him far more than the circling men. He had crouched at first, growing ever smaller within his windswept form, but he had been seen – he knew that and fidgeted slightly. He was ever watchful for the first lunge of the dog. They were shutting off an escape route, one of the few routes he knew really well, and it troubled him. Still he crouched, his heart beating madly, as it had before each and every chase in his trouble-filled life. The trio were over his escape run now, and they had stopped. Lepus became distressed, his hind legs twitching, his body ready for the lightning-quick lunge that would leave his pursuers far behind. His ears became erect, or nearly erect, for one still hung at a strange angle. He could not take this tension for long. He burst into flight.

It happened so quickly that Harvey sucked in his breath, uttering a quiet, hissing attempt at 'Jesus'. The dog had rocketed from the slip as the hare moved, and in a split second he had reached to strike. He struck, the strike that had won him the contest against the itinerants in Norfolk, the strike that had put an end to a hundred hares, his head moving like an enraged python. At the moment of impact, Lepus moved, half-rolling, half-jinking to avoid the bite. It was a move he had used to baffle a hundred dogs, a move that had ensured he would survive to breed a dozen leverets on the estate. He jinked, and the speeding dog overshot. Czar braked rapidly, bearing down on his left leg, losing scarcely a foot, and was on Lepus again, striking at him as he raced through the hollow of mist near to the lower reaches of the upper pastures. Twice Czar bowled him, twice Brennan smiled at the squeal of the hare, but each time Czar's head came up without the hare in his jaws. His teeth chopped at the crippled ear, tearing it slightly, bringing blood and a high-pitched, girl-like scream.

In the hollow, Lepus dodged and ducked beneath the layer of cotton-wool fog. He was old now, and tired, and his bones creaked slightly as he ran, desperately evading the adder-like thrusts of the dog. Yet the spirit that bubbled and boiled within the diminutive hare still lived and screamed not to expire in the crushing mouth of the dog. Lepus made heroic efforts to evade the great golden dog, efforts that would not have disgraced the hare in its prime, but the great yellow shape refused to quit, refused to be thrown off, refused to be outpaced. A dozen odd irregular twists Lepus made, but always Czar stuck to him as though they were joined by a short invisible thread. And again, at the point of impact when capture seemed certain, the hare disappeared in another mist-filled hollow.

Brennan watched the spectacle, enthralled by the duel of the two athletes. He had seen the tiny hare grow to maturity, heard stories of its legendary speed and turning ability, and now he was certain the legend would be brought to an end. He was aware of the age of the hare, aware of its fading speed, but the destruction of the creature drove all thoughts of fairness and 'law' from his mind. Harvey watched Brennan's anxious face, aware that in spirit Brennan was running with the dog, experiencing the same wild excitement, the same agony of muscle, the same exertion. Each time the dog struck, Brennan let loose a long, sibilant hiss – at each turn, Brennan's face creased with the sympathetic exertion for the chase. The protagonists had now left the misty hollow and were racing for the gate at the lower pastures towards the sea of whiteness in the water meadows. Momentarily they disappeared from sight as they crossed the horizon and vanished towards the mist.

There was nothing to indicate what had happened. There was simply a thud, a choked and strangled scream and the sound of running ceased. Brennan sprinted across the horizon to the patch of thick, icy mist that obscured the gateway. Lying across the foot of the gate was Czar, his head turned at a hideous angle, a strut of the oak gate smashed in two by the force of the collision. He gazed at the inert dog, unable to believe what had happened, then he fell to the ground, touching the still-twitching body. A strangled gasp escaped from his mouth, but 'Bastard!' was all the sense that emerged from the gasp as tears of rage rolled down his face.

Harvey walked to the kneeling man and touched his arm as gently as he would a maid's. 'Go home, Brennan, I'll see to the dog,' he whispered softly.

In the water meadows Lepus had stopped running and was browsing on some dead grass, chinning the frosted ragwort. He extracted a wet faecal pellet and ambled into the mist.

Thus the hare for his sin of vanity was cursed to race his way for ever until the end of eternity, or until God shall tire of his sport of shape-making and call all things back into the Abyss whence they came.

—LEPUS RUNS FOREVER— (J.H.)

Finale.